EARL OF SUSSEX

WICKED EARLS' CLUB

TAMMY ANDRESEN

Copyright © 2017 by Tammy Andresen

All rights reserved.

No part of this book may be reproduced in any form or by any electronic or mechanical means, including information storage and retrieval systems, without written permission from the author, except for the use of brief quotations in a book review.

❧ Created with Vellum

PROLOGUE

*L*uke Bentley, Earl of Sussex, strolled up to the nondescript brick front building, and stopped to glance at its exterior. He did this nearly every time he arrived. It was miraculous to him that something so outwardly plain could hold such delights within. The only indication of what this building held was the emblem emblazoned on the door, a single *W* inlaid in gold. This same mark was pinned to the lapel of his waistcoat.

A slow wicked grin spread across his lips. He loved that this building could appear so nondescript but be full of decadent sin. Such was true for females as well. One never knew what woman might bloom in his arms, revealing secret delights at which her perfectly groomed exterior barely hinted.

That was why he rarely turned away a woman. Well, one of the reasons, anyway. He had other less noble motivations for his endless parade of lovers. But he digressed.

Before him was his most favorite place in London, perhaps all of England…The Wicked Earls' Club. It had once been The Earls' Guild or some such foppery, but over the years it had turned into a haven for men like him. It allowed men of means and title to relax with a drink and some cards, perhaps a woman, without the prying eyes of society.

The members never spoke of the club or its existence outside of these walls in order to keep the utmost secrecy. In this way, they could continue with their delicious debauchery for as long as they chose. Luke planned on gracing its halls forever.

There were a few rules, not written of course, but understood. Once a man married, for example, his invitation to the club was rescinded. At such a time, he could find a proper, public gentlemen's club to drink his scotch. Luke ran a hand through his hair. But matrimony was an unfortunate state he planned never to find himself in. It was also the reason for his visit.

The building was located at 276 Bedford Place, on the outskirts of respectable London. It allowed for men of his guild to come here without fear of being seen in an unseemly place while still being close to other delights of London's less upstanding variety.

He inserted his key into the lock and turned it with a resounding click. Each member had his own nondescript key for entrance any time, night or day. He entered the darkened foyer and closed the door, locking it behind him.

He knew this entrance like his own bedroom, and moved easily down the hall, despite the darkness.

As he turned the corner, a room opened to his left. It was well-lit and extravagantly decorated, not in the way a woman might prefer, but perfect for a man. It was Luke's second home. Rich leather chairs abounded, as did decanters of the finest scotch, brandy, and whiskey, the best a man could hope to drink. Several waiters and a maître d' stood at the ready to grant any whim he should seek.

Today he wished most to discuss a particularly vexing dilemma he had with two of his closest compatriots, Lord Gracon and Lord Harrington.

He found them seated in a quiet corner, perfect for private

conversation. Though it was not yet ten in the morning, he stopped to pour himself a tall snifter of scotch. He'd already been to his boxing club this morning and could use the fortification for what he was about to say.

Normally, he boxed in the afternoons, his late-night activities making noon his normal rising time. But his father insisted Luke stay in last night, so he had risen early and left the house as soon as possible.

While he loved his parents, their visits were often fraught with tension, this one being the most difficult yet. The Marquess of Winston was a man who demanded his own way.

"So what brings you here at such an early hour?" Lord Gracon took a sip of tea, eyeing him over the rim.

"You know my mother and father are in town." Luke grimaced at the words.

"Are they staying at Clearwater?" Lord Harrington asked.

"No. They chose to stay with me instead."

"How…" Gracon paused. "Unfortunate."

Luke ran his hand through his hair again. It was a gesture to which he was not normally prone. "You don't know the half of it."

"Enlighten us." Harrington grinned.

It was better to just say the words and have it be out. "They want me to marry." He grimaced, went to take a swig of his scotch, and found his stomach couldn't tolerate it. Setting the glass down again, he ran his fingers through his hair again.

"Well, that is most distressing." Gracon raised his cup to his lips again, but Luke had the distinct impression that he hid a smile with his teacup.

"It gets worse." He took a breath, steadying himself. "They've made a match. Without my consent."

Both men leaned forward then, cups set to the side, matching grins on their faces. "Who?" Gracon asked.

Damnation, they weren't even trying to hide their glee. "Lady Tabitha Riley." He spit the words. During the few balls his parents had forced him to attend, he had never seen the lady in question, though his father had assured him she was there. He had replied that if she were worth seeing, he would have, in fact, already met her.

"What's to complain about there, old chap?" Harrington leaned over and slapped him on the back. "She's quite pretty, well connected, very sweet. She'll make an excellent wife."

Gracon nodded in agreement but Luke slashed his hand through the air. "I don't want a wife. And if I did, she'd be the last woman I picked."

"Last…really? You'd marry Lady Millicent Dunphry first?" Gracon grinned.

Harrington, catching on to the game, laughed. "Or Lady Mildred Cleary?"

Luke stared at them unamused. "You're supposed to be helping me. Not poking fun. She's a first-rate wallflower. I bet she goes to bed by exactly eight every evening and rises with the sun. She most likely has excellent embroidery skills and talks endlessly about gossip. I will be dead by the age of forty, having perished from complete boredom."

Gracon sighed and sat back in his chair. "If you married the type of woman you normally cavort with, you'd depart us at the ripe old age of thirty-five. My friend, you could stand with a little more stability."

Luke made to protest but Gracon raised his hand.

"Besides, you are the one who is so fond of saying that the outside wrapping doesn't reveal what is underneath. Perhaps you should meet Lady Tabitha first before you judge."

Well, blast it all to hell…using his own words against him. Luke doubted any woman could convince him to marry. But, all the same, he supposed the man had a point.

CHAPTER 1

ne week later:

LADY TABITHA SAT PERCHED on the end of her chair in her father's study and attempted to keep her mouth from hanging open. She was fairly certain her father had just told her that marriage contracts were being drawn up with the Earl of Sussex.

"You can't be serious?" she mumbled before she could stop herself.

"I can assure you, I am as serious as the plague, young lady," her father, The Duke of Waverly replied.

Barreling headlong into disaster, she let the words tumble from her lips. "But Papa, he is a known rake and debaucher, drinking and gambling and…"

"Stop, darling. A lady does not say such things." Her mother lifted a kerchief to her mouth.

"Of course, Mother. I apologize." She took a breath. "I have no illusions of a love match, but I thought perchance, I might at least share some common interests with my future bridegroom."

"Don't be ridiculous, of course you have common interests. You're both members of the peerage, from excellent families, with a common goal to populate the next generation of—" Her mother was now waving the kerchief, apparently *populating the next generation* had her more excited than Tabbie had seen her in quite some time.

"Yes, dear. Thank you. We need not discuss that part yet." Her father turned back to her. "I hear he is quite handsome. You should meet him before you dismiss him."

"We've already met." Her lips thinned into a straight line. That was to say, she had been introduced to him on two separate occasions but always his eyes had barely grazed her before they were following some other woman about the room. No man had ever made her feel so invisible and she was a wallflower, or she would be if she weren't the daughter of a duke.

"Excellent. They are arriving today for a visit. I expect you to have your afternoon tea together."

"I beg your pardon?" She stood, forgetting her manners completely. "Today?"

"Sit down." Her father's stern voice reverberated through the room.

She had no choice but to do as she was told. But her eyes narrowed. Her father must have known they were coming for some time. He'd intentionally kept this information from her. Most likely so that she didn't have time to scheme her way out of it.

"You'll be on your best behavior. You'll be polite and agreeable. You will keep quiet or, if you speak, you will keep your tongue sweet."

"What is that supposed to mean?" Her own anger was rising.

"Tabbie, darling, you have a tendency to make men feel lesser when you verbally..." Her mother paused but her father filled in.

"Assault them." He gave a nod to emphasize his point.

"That is ridiculous. I don't—"

"Oh darling, you're one of the kindest people I know. But you do have a bit of a temper. And the words that you speak when in those fits…" Her mother covered her mouth with her hand.

"To smart for your own good," her father mumbled.

"Find someone else." Tabbie stood again.

"There's no one else. Your decision to stay next to the wall for every soiree we attend has made it difficult to find a suitor." Her father stood too. "Be polite."

"Fine," she murmured. Tabbie lifted her skirts and exited the office with as much dignity as she could muster. She still had several hours before they were to meet. Surely she could come up with a plan before then.

Three hours later, she sat in the parlor awaiting the Earl of Sussex. The blasted man was late. He was supposed to have arrived at half past two but it was now three and he was nowhere to be seen. In want of something to do, she picked up a book sitting artfully on the table. *History of Ducal England* graced the spine and she tried not to roll her eyes.

"Interesting reading," a baritone voice rumbled from the door. It was melodious in a way that struck a chord deep within her. But she ignored the feeling, preferring to focus on the issue at hand.

Appeal was not something he lacked, unlike herself. The few balls they both attended, she couldn't help but see him. Dark wavy hair, longer than fashionable, was swept back to show strong cheekbones and piercing green eyes. Broad shouldered, he stood a head taller than near every other man she'd met. But she couldn't let good looks distract her now. "Do you like it, my lord? I thought some light reading might temper my boredom. So kind of you to keep me waiting."

The distinct clink of her chaperone's embroidery needles knocking together filled the room then stopped completely. Her father would hear of her comment, no doubt. A second later, the needles resumed their tempo of work and a small chuckle fell from the earl's lips.

"A pleasure, I'm sure, my lady," he murmured.

The dolt wasn't going to take the bait. Well, two could play at that game. "Charmed, I'm sure." Without waiting for his response, she set down the book and got up, moving to the window, her back to him.

Drat it all, but she was keenly aware of his presence as he walked up behind her. "So," his voice floated over her skin, causing her to shiver. "We're to be married."

"So it would seem." She kept her eyes trained on the garden but his hand came to rest on the glass just next to her, obstructing her view and his body leaned in so close she could feel his heat. If she hadn't been certain he was a rake before, she knew it now. No gentleman would take such liberties.

"*Seem?* You don't think we'll marry?" There was a laugh in his voice. "Well, this *is* an interesting twist."

"Do you want to marry me?" They were getting to the heart of things rather quickly. Tabbie took a deep breath. It was important to make herself clear.

"Please don't take it personally. I don't want to marry anyone." His breath tickled her ear. It would truly help if he backed up.

"I understand entirely," she replied, and she did. A rake was as unappealing to her as a wallflower likely was to him. Though she appreciated him not coming out and saying it.

"But an earl would make a good catch for you, so I am puzzling out your resistance." His hand brushed the small of her back in a gesture that was entirely inappropriate and ruining her concentration.

Picking her next words carefully, she took a deep breath. "I make no assumption that I shall find love, but I would prefer a husband that wanted my company."

"Lady Tabitha, turn around," he commanded. She hesitated for a second and then it was as though her feet had a mind of their own as she turned to finally look at him. Catching her breath, her eyes devoured his face. He was even more handsome this close with strong cheekbones and full lips that tilted in the slightest smile. They looked soft and enticing and she reached her gloved hand up as though to touch her fingers to them.

She was a woman who always had her wits about her. But in this moment, she couldn't put a single thought together as he too assessed her.

"Now we are having an actual conversation." One of his eyebrows arched up.

"Really? I preferred when I faced the window," she mumbled, lowering her hand. She blinked and looked away, trying to call her wayward body back to heel.

"And why is that?" His voice was so close. His lips enticing as they twitched with amusement.

"Must every woman in England tell you?" She turned away again.

SURPRISE RIPPLED through Luke for at least the third time since he had entered the room. Lady Tabitha was a known wallflower, that was a fact, but how could she be that blasted pretty and not be noticed? Granted her features erred on the side of sweet rather than seductive, luminous blue eyes, thick wavy auburn hair that looked barely contained by pins. He wondered what it might look like spread across a crisp white pillow.

Her nose was tiny and adorable with a little sprinkling of freckles. He had the distinct urge to kiss each one as he counted them. As she stood facing the window, he assessed the curve of her backside, which he declared delightfully perfect.

While she wasn't tall, as was currently in fashion with the *ton*, she looked just the right size to fit against him, her curves softening his hard edges in all the best ways.

He tried to decide what he might ask her first. What should every woman in England tell him? He already knew Lady Tabitha was referring to his looks. But what had she meant before about him not liking her? "Why would you think I wouldn't want your company?"

She turned back to him then, surprise written on her adorable features. "I would have thought it obvious."

"To you perhaps, but I would enjoy being enlightened." His hand drifted to her hip. It was less than appropriate but he couldn't seem to stop himself. Despite being a known rake and a member of the Wicked Earls' Club, he had boundaries. He kept his attention to women who understood what it meant for a man to be a rake. Widows, light skirts, and the like. Generally, he stayed far away from young ladies of marriageable age. And when forced into their company, he kept his hands firmly to himself. The last thing he needed was to encourage a marriage-minded mama.

He asked himself why Lady Tabitha was different. Perhaps because he thought they would marry after all? But no, that wasn't it. It seemed to be that he wanted to touch her. He couldn't remember the last time he desired to touch a woman this much.

"Well, I am a wallflower to begin. Everyone knows it."

"You chose to be so. Leaving balls as early as possible, declining dances until men stopped asking. Flaying the few men who persist with your tongue."

"That was only Lord Carrington. He was rather rude." Her chin tilted up to a jaunty angle and he had to grin.

She had real spirit. Luke couldn't help but admire it. He wondered if she would be this feisty in bed. Delicious heat curled in his loins at the thought.

"Good for you. Now continue, why wouldn't I want your company?"

"Well, I spend my time feeding the homeless and helping at orphanages." She raised her eyebrows, as though that meant something. Her hand came to her other hip. Even with his large hand encircling her waist, she had spirit. He found that he liked it immensely.

"Yes?" His voice rumbled and he saw color rise in her cheeks. What was she thinking?

"What do you spend your days doing, my lord?"

Surprise again flitted across his features. The little chit was judging him. What was more, she had found him to be lacking. It was he who was supposed to reject her. "Why you little…"

"Tut tut." She raised her finger between them and he had the absurd urge to kiss it, lick it. Mayhap give it a little nibble. "You don't want to marry me either, remember."

"With a tongue like that—" he started but he saw the hurt cross her face. Her luscious lips turned down at the corners, her eyes crinkled and her shoulders dropped. Then she straightened back up. He admired her tenacity and a little guilt wiggled through him that he had made her feel such. Truly he didn't mind a little banter; in fact, he quite enjoyed it. A woman with no spark would be dull indeed and he shouldn't have said it.

"But you're right about neither of us wanting to marry. What do you propose?"

Her frown turned to a glowing smile in a second and he basked in its radiance. It lit her face, making him smile in return. "I'm so glad you agree. I can't ruin our relationship. I'll never socially recover. But you, you're a known rake. You could be caught tupping a maid or—"

His body clenched and damn it all to hell if his cock didn't swell at the word tupping coming from her full sweet lips. If only he could tup her. The swell of her hips begged for his other hand. "Did you just suggest I tup a maid?"

"Yes, but you must be caught." She gave him an eager nod.

"This is your plan?" His eyebrows lifted as he assessed her.

One of her fingers rested on her bottom lip as she considered him. He wanted to replace that finger with his mouth. But she seemed unaware of how she was affecting him as she spoke. "My parents only told me of your visit this morning. I am sure they didn't want me to have much time for planning."

His eyebrows rose higher. "Do you scheme often?"

"Only when necessary." Her tone implied that should be obvious. He tried to hide his grin. Damned if she wasn't interesting.

"You are a lady, how do you even know what tupping is?"

"You'd be amazed what you hear when by the wall." She gave him a grin. Her eyes danced with a merriment that was infectious.

"You do realize whatever maid I was caught with would be sacked." He crossed his arms then but immediately regretted it. He missed her heat under his hand, the feel of her body.

But he had to stop thinking this way. While this entire conversation had been far more entertaining than he'd ever dreamed possible, it would probably be best to put it to an end.

"Drat." Her little slippered foot stomped on the plush carpet. He'd like to see that foot, and the calf attached to it. Perhaps he'd slide her skirt higher up her thigh until he…

"Lady Tabitha, you've been over by that window for far too long. Please come back to the settee," her chaperone called.

"Keep thinking of ideas." Her gloved hand rested upon his lapel covering his pin emblazoned with the *W*. His body clenched again and his fingers itched to return to her hip. "We must come up with a plan quickly. Meet me in the library tonight at the stroke of twelve so that we may decide what to do."

It was a terrible idea. If caught, there would be no escaping marriage. But, it was also exceedingly fun and the last thing he had ever expected from this meeting today. And so, he was absolutely going.

CHAPTER 2

Dinner had been the exact affair he would have expected coming to a duke's country estate. A dull, tedious event full of bland conversation and, he had to admit, excellent wine.

Though when his glass had been refilled, he'd seen Lady Tabitha eye him over the table and give a subtle shake of her head. Blasted woman. They weren't even engaged yet and she was already limiting his alcohol.

But he set the glass down and excused himself from the table. Meeting her eyes as he reached the door, he crooked his finger at her.

Her eyes widened as she glanced around the table to see who might have noticed. But no one had.

Stepping into the hall, he waited for more than a few minutes until she joined him. "Have you gone mad?" she hissed as she reached his side. "We'll be married by the morning."

"You're being dramatic," he rolled his eyes. "Besides, you've married us in your mind anyway, telling me not to drink." He glared at her in accusation.

She gave a little shrug. It highlighted the soft curve of her creamy shoulder. He followed the neck of her dress to where there was just a hint of cleavage visible above the ivory fabric. He'd love to lick the spot just above it, then—

"I simply wanted you to have all your mental faculties this evening. It's both our futures at stake here."

Well, that was a bloody good point. But he didn't say it out loud. Instead, he stepped forward and whispered, "Just don't make a habit of it."

She reached out her hand and gave him the tiniest little push. Heat radiated from the spot where she touched him. "From what I hear, some moderation would be good for you."

His eyes narrowed and he snatched up her hand that had just touched him, his other coming to her waist. Her very tiny waist, small enough he was sure he could circle it with his hands. But he wouldn't be distracted now. What gossip was the *ton* saying about him? "What the bloody hell does that mean?"

She gave a little gasp and he wasn't sure if it was his question, the use of profanity, or the fact that he'd pulled her body close to his. But a little fire lit in her eyes as her mouth parted. It was stunning. All he need do was drop his head.

He heated, his body and his mind responding to the challenge before him. He felt anticipation course through him at what she might say next. She didn't disappoint. "Since it appears we've tossed out all rules of decorum, I'll speak plainly. Do you deny that you are a rake?" Her eyebrows shot up and her eyes widened in a way that made her resemble prey. Something akin to a growl rumbled deep within his throat. He wasn't offended. But speaking of his rakish ways, and the look on her face, made him long to practice them on her.

"I make no bones about the fact that I have enjoyed a few willing women." He pulled her completely against his body and the feel of her was delicious. Her soft curves molded to him in a way no other woman ever had.

But her mouth formed an O. "What are you doing?"

A chuckle erupted from his chest. "Relax, I said willing. Besides, I never dally with marriageable ladies."

Her fear was immediately replaced with disbelief. "Really, not even women like Lady Ravenna?"

"How in the bloody blue blazes did you know about that?" He pressed her closer even as he blinked in disbelief. Just when he thought he'd had the upper hand.

She waved her hand, turning away and pushing against his chest for distance. "You weren't exactly subtle, I'm sure."

He let her push away though he instantly regretted it. Questions bubbled up to his lips. He'd called her out here to chastise her on her bad behavior but somehow it was him who was being chastised. A grin played at his lips. It was delightful. She was interesting, intelligent, and beautiful and he wanted to know more. "None of that matters. We are talking about our future--"

"And that is why you need to keep from over imbibing. We'll never escape the marriage noose if we don't put our heads together."

That was an idea he liked immensely. Their heads together. He was about to tell her so when a movement at the door caught his attention.

A young lady stood in the doorway, with the same auburn hair and flashing eyes as Lady Tabitha. Gripping her hands together, she looked earnestly at her sister. "Tabbie, get back in here. Your absence has been noticed. Mother will have a fit if you don't—"

Lady Tabitha sighed. "I'm coming, Tricia." Then she turned back to him. "I will see you tonight."

Leaning down, he whispered in her ear, "You most certainly will, Tabbie."

TABBIE TRIED to concentrate on the rest of the evening. But she barely listened to any of the conversation filtering around her. It wasn't surprising to her that she was distracted. What was rather disconcerting was the cause. She should be dreaming up ways to escape this match not thinking about the feel of the earl's arms. *Luke*, she'd heard the marchioness, his mother, whisper at dinner when he'd finally returned from the hall. She hadn't sounded terribly pleased with her son.

It briefly occurred to her that she might just marry him. Let him touch her in all sorts of delicious ways. She'd felt the proof of his...*affection* when he'd held her close.

But that was a foolish idea that would only end in her heartbreak. He was a rake. He'd admitted it himself. Soon he would tire of her, only she wouldn't be able to walk away. She'd be forced to watch as he found a new lady upon whom he could lavish his affection. She would go back to being the wallflower that he looked through in favor of a more attractive woman. It would shatter her to be rejected by him again.

Shuddering, she closed her eyes. That was when she realized that the marquess was speaking to her. And she hadn't been paying attention at all. "Forgive me," she gave an apologetic smile.

"I've heard a great deal about the charity work you've been participating in," he repeated with a bland smile.

She was proud of the work she'd done. Recently, she opened a shelter for women and their children who'd lost or never had a provider. It kept them clothed and fed and, in return, the women mended laundry. It gave them a far better option than the workhouse they might otherwise have to endure. She'd seen those places. They were almost worse than death.

But she was adept at aristocratic conversation and she knew the man was simply being polite. She'd give him the briefest answer possible to excuse him from the discussion. "Thank you, my lord. It is very fulfilling."

She expected the marquess to nod and turn away but his eyes were intent upon her. "Will you keep up such activities after you are wed?"

It was a trap. There was something about her he wanted to

know. She was a candidate for his son. Of course his interest was more than casual.

Her father glared at her down the table, his warning to keep her tongue sweet ringing in her ears. With a sigh, she gave the expected answer rather than one she really wanted to say. "It will be up to my husband."

The marquess gave her a satisfied nod and then turned away, but Luke's eyes were intent upon her. One of his eyebrows rose in question and she ducked her head to keep from grinning.

It was as though they were having a silent conversation across the table, one where he understood the subtext of her comment, the person she was when she wasn't pretending to be the lady her parents wanted her to be.

They'd known each other for hours and yet he understood her already. How peculiar.

As dinner finished, the men retired to smoke and Tabbie prepared to wait until it was time for her midnight meeting.

Two hours later she debated changing out of her evening gown, but opted to leave it on. Luke would likely still be in his waistcoat, tailcoat, and cravat and she didn't want to be at a disadvantage. Her clothing would be like armor. If she were wearing it, this would seem like any other social engagement and not the clandestine meeting it resembled.

Though she had no untoward intentions. Unless, of course, scheming to end an engagement counted as untoward. Which it likely did. But she was not here for a tryst, no matter how handsome he was. Or how his lips tempted her. And certainly not because, despite having only known her for a few hours, he seemed to really see her, to understand who she was beneath the façade she presented as a duke's daughter.

Perching on a windowsill, she pushed open the glass and stared out at the night sky, a clear spring evening, the moon shining brightly into the room. It bathed her in a pale light and she turned her face up to it, enjoying the quiet this time of night brought.

Her eyes fluttered closed as she took a breath of damp air filtering in from the outside. It gave her a slight chill but in a way that was invigorating. She shivered and goosebumps started forming on her arms, but a smile touched her lips. Meeting with a handsome man to hatch a plot was so exciting.

The slightest noise behind her made her eyes flutter open but before she could even turn, a hand had enveloped her arm and warm breath blew across her cheek. "You look stunning like that, bathed in moonlight."

Luke. His hand was warm and strong, heating her skin. "That is likely because you lack for a better view."

"You doubt your own appeal?" His lips grazed her earlobe, sending shivers of a different kind entirely racing along her skin.

"To you? Most decidedly." Even on her best day she wouldn't keep the attention of a man like him for very long. Which was exactly why she had to focus on their plot to escape this engagement.

He didn't back up. If anything, he pressed closer. "You should give yourself more credit, my little Tabbie."

She turned to speak to him then. But he was so close and as her head twisted, their lips brushed together. It was soft and gentle and a complete accident. Still seated on the sill, she couldn't go very far, but she wrenched her head back. "I apologize. I didn't mean to—"

But her words were cut off as his head dipped back down, taking her lips again. This was not the soft brush of moments before, this was a claiming. Soft, yet firm lips pressed against hers, making her pulse race.

His lips left hers for a second only to press against hers again, over and over. Her chest rose and fell rapidly, as his hands drifted to her cheeks. His palms held her face as his fingers spread into her hair. Her own hands drifted to his chest, grasping fistfuls of his waistcoat. Without which, she was sure she would go spinning off the sill. His kisses had sent her body careening out of control.

He finally lifted his head and while part of her desperately wanted him to bring his lips back to hers, another saner part fought to gain control of her body. She swallowed. "What just happened?" she managed to croak out.

He was still so close, his hands holding her head, his lips only a few inches from hers. "I kissed you."

Her eyes focused in a little more. "I'm aware of that. I just didn't expect it to be so…" *Consuming.* That was the only word that might describe how she felt now. In this moment, she'd likely give him everything that was hers to offer if he'd only kiss her again.

"Was it better or worse than the kisses before it?" His eyes were narrowing and assessing her with an intensity that was alarming, as though her answer mattered.

"I…" Her cheeks heated. He knew she was a wallflower, but it still embarrassed her to admit the truth. "I don't have any experience with which to compare."

He made a sound, rough and masculine, deep in his throat. She didn't know what it meant but the next moment, he was pulling her up off the sill, wrapping her in his arms as his lips descended again. Over and over they claimed hers until he slanted them open and his tongue slid against hers. If she had heated before, she was aflame now and a moan escaped her lips to be swallowed by his.

His hands slid back up, skimming across her shoulders, brushing her neck, twining into her hair. Her insides ached with need and she pressed against him, the feel of his body increasing the torturous pleasure in the most delightful way.

And then his lips were gone. She blinked, trying to right the tilting room, wishing to find his kiss again. "I didn't know it would be like that." Was that her voice? So raspy and wanton?

"Neither did I." He was still holding her close, his hands in her hair, and his lips grazed her temple.

Her head snapped back, their eyes meeting, the haze of the kiss clearing. "You can't tell me you haven't kissed anyone. That is ridiculous."

His expression was forlorn as he seemed to drink her in with his gaze, devouring every detail. "When you are betrothed to your future husband and he kisses you, you will discover that not all kisses are created equal. When your bones don't melt and the room doesn't spin, you will understand that this kiss was special."

"How…how did you know that was how I responded?" Her eyes were round with wonder. Had he read her mind?

"I didn't. I was talking about me." He stepped away then, his face pained.

She nearly stumbled as he stopped supporting her and she grabbed the sill so she would remain on her feet. "Oh, I don't know what to say. I am sure other women have made you feel this way. I—"

"Tabbie." His voice was rough again, his breathing still ragged. "I am leaving tonight."

She blinked twice. What was he talking about? "Why? Was it the kiss? I didn't mean to. It won't happen again."

He shook his head. "I am going to find a woman. One who doesn't work here. We'll put her in a uniform for your plan. Your father will figure it out when he can't actually find the maid he needs to sack, but it will be too late by then."

"That's brilliant." Why hadn't she thought of that? Likely because she'd been daydreaming about his lips.

"I've hatched a few plots in my day." He leaned down and kissed her forehead. "I'll be back tomorrow afternoon. We can put our plan into action at the ball tomorrow night."

Well that was terribly efficient of him. She should be excited; it was her idea to begin with. But now, all she could feel was dread.

CHAPTER 3

*L*uke watched the sun rise and marveled at how much better it felt to stay up all night when he hadn't imbibed alcohol.

He was on the outskirts of London and though he longed to have this business done, he knew he should go to his townhouse and get a few hours' sleep. Then he could visit the club when it was closer to the noon meal. Several men would be there along with many of the ladies who were employed at the club. They were the kind of woman whose help he needed this evening.

Once he arrived home, his horse was led to the stable and he trudged up the stairs. His staff wasn't surprised to see him enter at dawn, his schedule was often erratic.

But because he hadn't been drinking, he noticed their averted eyes, and the way they efficiently avoided interacting with him.

His manservant waited in his room, ready to help him undress. While he guessed this was a regular duty for the man, undressing him at dawn, he didn't particularly want any company now. Something deep inside him was unsettled. "I'm not in need of your services this morning, Montgomery. Thank you, kindly."

Surprise was written all over Montgomery's face as he nodded and turned to leave.

Shame stabbed at Luke's chest. "Wait," he called.

"Yes, my lord?" Montgomery turned back to him.

"How often do you help me undress in the wee hours of the morning?" Luke's insides clenched as he waited for the answer.

"My lord?" Montgomery winced.

"It's all right, man. Just answer the question."

"Nearly every morning, sir," Montgomery slowly and quietly answered.

A sick feeling of dread and shame settled in his stomach. What had he become? "Thank you."

He finished undressing and lay in his bed. Looking over at the pillow next to him, he wondered what it might be like to have auburn curls trailing over the crisp white linen so that he could reach out and touch them. He pictured dancing blue eyes, sparkling with desire and intelligence, assessing him as creamy arms wrapped around his neck. Closing his own eyes, he let the fantasy wash over him. Her curves would fit perfectly against his side. He'd roll her over and kiss every inch of her glorious flesh. She'd cry his name as she shattered for him and then… Then he would hold her close. All night, she'd be pressed against him. Murmuring in her sleep, he'd hold and comfort her as he breathed in her scent.

He drifted to sleep, dreaming of Tabbie.

He woke with a start two hours later and grimaced at the empty pillow next to him. Giving himself a shake, he wondered what the bloody hell was wrong with him, dreaming of a woman so. It wasn't the desire that had him concerned. He'd pictured all sorts of women doing an array of sordid acts. Many of them had been played out in real life. It was the second half of his fantasy that shook him to his core. He wanted to bloody hold her close all night long. He never did that with anyone.

Bathing and dressing, he headed for the club, feeling unsettled and jumpy. Dread filled him. This time it wasn't thoughts of Tabbie but of finding another woman to touch that made him slightly ill. He only wanted to touch one woman and that scared him near to death.

He thought its walls might soothe him, but the usual feeling of calm did not come as he approached the club. He felt no joy in unlocking the door, no pleasure passing through the darkened hall.

Turning into the smoking room, he tossed himself into a recliner. Rubbing his eyes with his fingers, he tried to relax. Why was he so upset about finding a maid to tup? This was a normal occurrence for him. He must be losing his facilities wanting to be snuggled against Tabbie and not touch another female.

A drink arrived at the table on his right. It was his usual, a whiskey neat. Allowing his eyes to travel from the glass to the carrier, he took stock of the woman who had delivered it. Dark hair and luminous eyes stared back at him, a knowing smile rested on her lips. A day ago, he would have found that smile too tempting to resist. But now…it turned him cold. It was practiced, given to any handsome man who'd pay.

He wanted a woman who challenged him, who would give her love and affection to only him. No other. A woman like Tabbie. One who didn't give her smile knowingly to every handsome fellow who passed. But he pushed these thoughts aside. Tabbie would never be his and he needed to focus on the task at hand.

Ignoring the drink, he looked at the woman. "What's your name?"

"Mary." Her smile broadened, her hip taking on a flirty tilt as her hand rested on it. "Who are you then?"

"You can call me Luke." He gave her a half grin. He needed some modicum of charm. "Mary, I have a proposition for you."

"How much?" she asked, her eyes growing hungrier. Bloody hell, had they always been so obvious?

"Wouldn't you rather know what I'm going to ask first?" His eyebrows rose.

Shock made her eyes widen for a moment but then she recovered. "I know I don't have anything to worry about from the likes of you."

This woman needed to marry a man. Not him, of course. She had no sense whatsoever because if she had, she surely wouldn't say such ridiculous things. She didn't know him at all and there was no light of intelligence to suggest she had truly puzzled out the type of man he was. Tabbie would have eyed him with suspicion before she carefully questioned him to discover his true intentions.

He stood and whispered the plan, and her part, into her ear. To her credit, she looked rather skeptical till he mentioned the price. "I'll pay you a hundred gold pieces for the trouble."

Her eyes lit and her grin spread from ear to ear. "I'll do it." She nodded. "I can't believe you'll pay me that much and you don't even really want to have me, just pretend."

He kept the smile plastered on his face. He couldn't believe he'd ever found women like this attractive.

* * *

Tabbie paced in the library, her slippers muffling the sound of her footsteps tapping back and forth. He was late. Again.

The ball was in full swing downstairs, a welcome to his family. Everyone would be speculating about a match between the two of them. It was best to have this entire business done quickly.

The knob rattled and she stopped her pacing and stared at the door, her hands clutched together.

The door swung open. Luke, larger than life, filled the entrance. Her breath caught in her throat and her heart beat wildly. She clutched her hands tighter to keep from crossing the room and throwing her arms about him. "You're late."

"My apologies, my lady. Getting our mark here in a carriage proved a lengthy journey."

"Luke didn't tell me it would be so far." A woman's voice huffed behind him.

Tabbie's stomach dropped to her knees. The other woman had called him Luke. There was a piece of her that had wanted to believe that he had been a rake in the past but the present and future could be different. Now that she knew him, she could see a good man. A man that made her feel alive, attractive, and understood.

But his name on another woman's lips shattered any hope she may have been harboring. It spoke of intimacy and a relationship. The present was not just about the two of them like she wanted to believe. Her time with him would always be shared with other women. How many times would his name be uttered by some other female's lips? An emotion she barely recognized rose like bile, clogging her throat.

Her lips pressed together and she shoved a bundle of garments at him. "I'll be back with my father in twenty minutes." Then she made to walk out the door.

"How am I supposed to get Mary into these clothes?" he huffed, holding onto Tabbie's arm to stop her from breezing past him.

"I am sure a man such as yourself can figure it out." Her words held a resentment she barely recognized but she could see understanding dawning in his eyes.

"Tabbie." His voice was soft and then he pulled her close, his lips pressing against her ear. "Don't leave me alone with her. I'm begging you."

The ache inside of her eased considerably and all at once; she recognized that she'd been jealous. It had never happened before. She'd never been jealous of her friends, never even experienced sibling rivalry. Not even with her little brother, Theodore, or Teddy, as the family called him. Heir to the dukedom, he had long been the favorite, but rather than be jealous, she doted on him as everyone else did.

"You've been alone with her. You'll have to be alone with her in order to tu—"

"Don't say it." His jaw clenched. Then he was pulling her over to the other side of the room, leaving Mary to stand in the doorway staring at them. He turned his back on Mary so that Tabbie was completely shielded from the other woman's blatant stare. "Seven hours I spent in the carriage with her. In that time, she prattled endlessly and managed to say absolutely nothing."

His face was scrunched as though he'd smelled something awful. But Tabbie closed her eyes. He was drawing her back in. Making her forget what she already knew about him. She needed to remind herself what type of man he really was. "Surely you could think of something else to do with her? You had seven hours and considering she climbed in a carriage with you, I am sure she is more than willing."

He stilled, not even breathing. The only movement was the tightening of his hand around her upper arm. Finally he muttered, "Pardon?"

She didn't open her eyes, couldn't look at him. She would lose all resolve if she did. Instead, she barreled ahead. "You're going to be intimate with her anyway. Why not?"

His body pressed against hers. "Spend five minutes with her and you will know why not. That woman doesn't have a lick of sense or a grain of intelligence. Even I would not—"

"Wouldn't you?" Jealousy was rising again. Her first meeting with Luke, at the Winthrop's ball, he had looked right through her, focusing on Lady Ravenna instead. Coincidentally she was now Lady Winthrop but that marriage didn't happen for a few years. That ball, the hussy had been entirely focused on the Earl of Sussex, Luke.

But the second introduction Tabbie had been given to Luke, only six months prior, he had been smitten with a truly lovely blonde who could barely keep a thought in her pretty head. "Lady Ashford does not strike me as a woman with either sense or intelligence." Her breath hissed out.

"Open your eyes, Tabbie." His voice commanded and once again she obeyed. His eyes were roving her face as though searching for answers. They finally locked on her and his gaze was appraising, searching, searing. "Why those two women? You brought up Ravenna last night and now Lady Ashford." he finally asked.

"What does it matter?" She wrenched her arm from his grasp, breaking the gaze they had been locked in. She needed distance between them because her mind was too addled to think properly. Grasping her skirt, she swished away. "I will be back with my father in twenty minutes."

She ignored the tears pricking at her eyes as she hurried past the maid, Mary. Or whoever the woman was. This had all gotten so complicated. If only he hadn't kissed her. Or better still, it didn't affect her. He didn't affect her.

Finding her father was alarmingly easy. Even amongst the crush of people her father stood a head taller than most. He came stalking toward her. It turned out, he had been searching for her. "Where have you been?" he hissed.

Her hands shot to her hips. "Trying to sort out a problem you refuse to acknowledge."

Normally he would have lectured her on speaking her thoughts but instead his lips thinned. "And what problem is that?"

"The fact that the man you want to marry me to is renowned for chasing light skirts."

He huffed a breath. "The world is rarely fair, Tabbie. Men are beasts; their wives just don't know it. I've told you more than once, you're too smart for your own good. I meant it."

Her mouth hung open as she gazed at her father in astonishment. "Papa, you're not referring to yourself?" She hadn't called him that in some time, but the conversation had thrown her off guard.

"Of course I am not. I am simply trying to make the point that with arranged marriages, it is more often the case than you might think." He stepped closer. "I saw you both at the table last night. He understands you, Tabbie. He is handsome and well connected. You could do far worse."

If her mouth could have dropped lower still, it surely would have. But it was unladylike to stand there gaping so she snapped it closed. It was on the tip of her tongue to insist that she could do far better. A man who was faithful to her. But arguing wouldn't make her point and so she gestured for her father to follow. Her insides railed at having to suffer more of the feelings he seemed to provoke. Not the excitement but the jealousy and hurt that he caused. "This way." She waved her hand and turned back to the library, praying that she'd given Luke enough time to set up the ruse.

She walked slowly, a sick dread making her legs feel leaden. Even knowing what she would likely see didn't lesson her feelings of nausea. She would witness firsthand Luke holding another woman. Her father's strides matched hers. "What is this about?" he demanded.

Summoning her courage, she spoke. "I know that men have discreet affairs. When you spend most social gatherings by the wall, you hear a great deal. But there is a difference between discreet and flagrant." They had reached the library door. It had only been a quarter hour and she prayed that they were ready.

She gestured for her father to enter. She couldn't bring herself to open the door as her stomach twisted painfully.

Grimacing at her, he turned the knob and strode confidently into the room. "Sussex," she heard him grumble.

"Your Grace," Luke replied. There was no hint in their voices that anything was amiss. Which was perplexing. Tabbie inched closer to the opening and grabbing the jam, peeked around the door into the room. There was no sign of Mary. Instead, Sussex sat behind her father's desk looking at several sheets of paper. Deep down inside, relief washed over her. It was quickly replaced with confusion.

Her father turned back to her. "What is the meaning of this?"

Her mouth closed and then opened and then closed again. But try as she might, no response came out. She couldn't very well say that she had arranged for Luke to be caught with another woman. "I thought…that is to say…I assumed that…" she stuttered out, unable to formulate a thought. What had happened to their plan?

"Lady Tabitha has a rather low opinion of me, Your Grace." Luke cocked an eyebrow, apparently completely at ease.

"I am aware," her father responded drily. "Why are you in my library and why does Tabbie know that fact?"

"I followed him." Her mind finally snapped into action. Perhaps she could salvage this encounter after all. "He came in here with a maid."

Luke glowered at her. "I confess it is true. I hoped to sneak a glass of your brandy. I thought better of it."

Her father crossed his arms over his chest. "But you saw fit to look at my personal papers?"

Luke looked down then and Tabbie tensed. While she wanted Luke to be caught with the maid so that her father would end his pursuit of the engagement, she did not want him in trouble for anything else. "The marriage contracts." Luke gestured to the papers before him. "Forgive me. They so intimately involved me, that I could not resist."

Up to that moment, Tabbie had been numb, perplexed. Perhaps confused. But anger coursed through her. He had hoodwinked her while she had been attempting to trick her father. She wanted answers. But none would be had now and so, turning on her heel, she stomped out of the library.

CHAPTER 4

*L*uke strode through the ballroom, making his third circle. He was searching for that little minx, and had been unable to find her.

He needed to talk to her, immediately. Several things had taken unexpected turns this evening. For one, he couldn't lay a finger on Mary no matter how hard he tried. That had never happened to him before.

As if that wasn't strange enough, he'd read the marriage contract, and found it…pleasing.

A sniffling was the first indication that he was getting close, though he proceeded with caution in case it wasn't her. But a peek through a potted fern confirmed that it was his Tabbie, sitting alone, hiding behind a plant.

HE STEPPED around it and her eyes snapped to his as she swiped at her tears. Without missing a beat she stood. "You ruined the plan."

"I know." He gave a little shrug.

"Why?" she asked.

"I'm not entirely sure." He gave her a small smile. "I found the idea of touching her revolting."

"Oh," she responded her eyes going wide. "You did choose her."

She looked glorious in the moonlight that filtered through the bay of windows behind her. By day, she was stunning, but at night she was a moon goddess. Unable to help himself he reached for her hand and pulled her close. He kept his back to the throngs of people, the plant blocking much of their bodies so they had privacy. Her body molded to his in the most gratifying way. "The problem I seem to be having is that I don't want to touch anyone but you."

It was the truth. He thought his words might soften her further but they had the opposite effect. She stiffened and began to pull away. "You've only known me a day. Give it time. Some other lady will catch your fancy."

His own eyes narrowed. He was sensing a theme, something simmering below the surface. "You're correct. We've only known each other a day. Perhaps you have no idea what I may or may not do."

"No, you are incorrect. I have met you on multiple occasions prior to yesterday. I know precisely how you will proceed."

That made his head snap back. "You mean you've seen me at social events?"

Her face scrunched up in pain. It made his chest ache seeing her hurt like that. But he also knew he wouldn't at all like what she was about to say. "My lord, we've been introduced three times, including yesterday."

His mouth fell open and he stared as she moved back out of his arms, pressing against a window. "The other two times, you were too busy with your current infatuation to even acknowledge my presence. And while I am flattered to have made the list, I am aware that your interest is fleeting. Painfully so."

She started to walk away but he came to his senses and grabbed her hand, pulling her back behind the fern. Because now he understood all those references to his rakish ways and the true reason she was so against their marriage. He had inadvertently rejected her.

But he had a decision to make. He wanted her to know that she was different from those women. Special because she was so much more than just attractive or available. She was everything he could ever want in a partner. The question was, did he want a partner?

As he looked down into her eyes, made silver by the moonlight, he knew that he did. He wanted her, his moon goddess, in his bed every night and by his side every day. But how to convince her that those other women had been meaningless compared with her? "Tabbie," he took a breath as he fitted her back against himself. "I won't scheme with you to end our impending engagement any longer."

She took a hissing breath and attempted to jerk back out of his grasp but he was ready for it and he held her fast. Her eyes shot daggers at him. "You don't want to marry me. You will tire of me in a month and then I will have to watch as you ogle the new Lady Ravenna."

"I do want to marry you. And there will be no Lady Ravenna. There never was, by the way, a Lady Ravenna in my life. I told you, I have standards. And even though she was well known for her trysts prior to and after marriage, I don't touch unwed ladies of a marriageable age."

"But I saw you, your eyes were all over her." Tabbie's voice was sharp as though she were growing desperate.

"I was trying to figure out how to delicately remove myself from the situation she was attempting to put me in." He looked her straight in the eye, hoping that she might see the truth.

"Are you going to tell me the same is true with Lady Ashford?" Her lip curled as she bent as far away from him as her body would allow.

He wasn't going to allow her to put that much distance

between them. Bending down he whispered softly in her ear. "I never denied that I was a rake. What I need you to understand is that there is a world of difference between what I felt for Lady Ashford and what I feel for you. There is no confusing the two."

She shivered in his arms and he pulled her closer.

"If I believe you, then it is my heart that is at risk and once we are married, it can not be undone. Even if you break my heart, we are tied together."

He grimaced. She was right. All the risk was hers to bear. "I understand. I am not asking you to commit to the engagement. In fact, I will put it off as long as I can. I only ask that you not actively try to stop it so that I may have time to prove myself worthy of your affection."

He felt her still against him and then relax into him, her face softening. Wanting to kiss her, he resisted, opting to graze his lips across her forehead and then bend lower to touch his nose to hers.

Her breath caught. "What do you mean, prove your affection?"

"I will show you that my feelings are based on your wit, charm, and depth of character. Though it does help that you look like a goddess in the moonlight."

"Goddess?" she squeaked.

Luke smiled. Because while he was attempting to prove that he wasn't a rake, it wouldn't hurt to use a touch of his rakish charm. It had tempted many a lady. "Undoubtedly a goddess," he whispered. "But what will keep me entertained over a lifetime is your undeniable ability to keep me on my toes."

* * *

TABBIE LOOKED into the depth of his eyes, desperately wanting to believe him. This was the man who had looked through her on more than one occasion. But he had also seen her in ways so few had. Her body tingled at his touch. "I want to believe you," she whispered back. Which was a dangerous admittance. It revealed how much she cared.

"Have you participated in the ball at all this evening?" he asked, grinning.

"Hardly." She kept her eyes from rolling toward the heavens. "I hate them."

"Me too," he confessed with a wink.

He didn't mean that. They seemed like an affair a rake would want to participate in.

"You're lying."

"I've told you already. I avoid ladies of a marriageable age like the plague. Besides, I prefer more quiet, intimate activities." His lips brushed against hers then. It was scandalous. The tingling concentrated in the pit of her stomach, the juncture between her legs aching.

"But let's go make an appearance on the dance floor, shall we? This soiree is for us, after all. People will start to wonder."

"Perhaps they will wonder about you," her voice was breathier than she'd intended. "People rarely miss me."

He gave her a grin. "Fools." His grin spread. "But their loss is my gain." And then he was pulling her back toward the throng of dancers.

She hissed as his hand came to her waist. "You can't do this."

"Oh, I can." He winked. "I'll fill in your dance card after."

"You've got your arm around me as though we're already—" Her voice was breathy as they entered the throng of dancers and he pulled her into his arms.

"You'll have to get used it." He gave her a devilish grin. "I don't stand on ceremony."

One of her eyebrows lifted. That was the problem, now wasn't it? "I am aware that you like to flaunt the rules."

Spinning her around, he leaned far closer than was decent. "Still worried about my fidelity."

"What lady in my position would not be?"

"I have not married because I didn't want a monogamous relationship. I believe in the sanctity of marriage. It is a bedrock of our society. But once I do marry, I will not break my oath."

She bit her lip. What she hadn't realized in her prior meetings with Luke was how very intelligent he was. He was correct in that there was much she didn't know about him. And while some tiny voice cried that she was going to get hurt, a much louder one was thrilled by the prospect of deepening her relationship with this handsome, intelligent man who was saying everything she needed to hear.

Though she certainly wasn't ready to commit to marriage. He was still a rake and she would do well to remember that fact. It was just that he muddled her thoughts so and made her want to believe him. It was so dangerous.

As the dance ended, he placed her hand in the crook of his arm and then walked her back to her mother's side. Her mother looked livid, and Tabbie knew she would be in a great deal of trouble for all the time she'd spent not attending the ball.

Luke made a show of filling a second spot on her dance card and then attempted to write his name on a third. She yanked the card away, then realized how unladylike her own behavior was. What a pair they made. If they were a pair, which they most decidedly were not.

He gestured to some chairs nearby. "I know how winded you are, my lady. If you'd like to sit this next dance out, I will be happy to attend you."

She bit back a smile and nodded her head. She was not at all winded but he was claiming another dance for himself in his own fashion.

As they moved toward the chairs, she mumbled, "Keep your hands to yourself."

"Not a chance." He grinned back.

She warmed at his words because having him look upon her

like this was like the sun shining down on her after a long cold winter. How long until winter returned?

He was discreet, at least. He kept his touches light and not easily seen. Every subtle brush made her skin catch on fire anew. She couldn't stand much more. She'd forget her resolve and throw herself into his arms.

Standing, Tabbie tried to come up with an excuse, any reason to join her mother and stand by the wall. Her emotions were a jumble, this evening having been more eventful than she could have imagined.

But he stood too. "Where do you think you're going?"

Her mouth opened as she searched for words.

"There you are, my lady." Lord Crummell approached from her left. "We don't want to miss our set." He held out his arm to her.

Deep and low, a noise not unlike a growl rumbled in Luke's throat. She saw his fingers flex and she flicked him a view of her dance card. "He asked earlier this evening, before the library."

That did not seem to still Luke's rumblings but rather amplify them. "Tell him you're too tired to dance."

"I shan't. It would be rude." She sniffed then turned toward Lord Crummell.

Luke leaned in low. "You don't want to share me, but I don't share well either. You're mine now, Tabbie. Only mine."

"Since when?" she huffed, ignoring Crummell.

"Since the library. I've made a decision and so…"

She took a half step closer, irritation bubbling to the surface. "Well, I haven't. I'm still deciding." Then she turned on her heel and marched over to Crummell.

The dance was in stark contrast to the one she shared with Luke for several reasons. Lord Crummell's movements were insecure, hesitant, and left them bumping into one another in a most embarrassing fashion. He didn't have the commanding presence that Luke had. Tabbie tried to ignore it and enjoy herself but it was difficult to forget.

As if that weren't enough, Luke stalked around the dance floor, looking like a large animal sighting its prey.

And other partygoers noticed his behavior. Their eyes travelled from her to him, gloved hands covering their mouths to whisper to one another.

It made her flush with embarrassment and…desire. She had seen him appraise another woman, but those had been discreet. She had only noticed because he'd been ignoring her. But this. No one in the room could mistake what he wanted. *Her.*

Crummell, already out of sorts, nearly tripped over his own feet as Luke stalked closer.

She was leading now, and pulling Crummell through the steps, praying for the dance to end. This evening had left her mind spinning, and she desperately needed some solitude to sort it all out. She knew that she should not allow Luke to affect her so, but his presence, as always, was overwhelming her, making her forget the good sense she was born with.

Part of her desperately wanted to believe that he really did feel differently about her then the women of his past, but how could she trust in that so soon? It was foolish.

Blessedly, the music ended and Crummell returned her to her mother's side. But he had hardly bowed before Luke was next to her again, pulling her onto the floor.

Her mother's eyes were wide as Luke tucked her hand into his elbow. "This is our dance, is it not?"

"It is not," she answered breathlessly. "And you are doing this on purpose."

"Tabbie," he leaned down to speak close to her ear. "I will confess to being a man who knows what he wants."

She closed her eyes. It was so tempting to get swept away. She'd like to allow him to kiss her again until she forgot even her own name. "You are terrible."

As their dance ended, Tabbie became aware that they had caught, not only the attention of most of the party, but of their fathers as well. The duke and marquess stood on the outskirts of the dancers watching their children with intent eyes.

As they passed by, her father met Luke's eyes. "See me first thing in the morning."

Luke gave a nod and then escorted her back to her mother. "We can't dance again," she whispered.

"I know. But I won't be far."

CHAPTER 5

Luke crossed his arms as he stared across the desk at the duke. His father sat next to him, the marquess's face set in a frown. Luke ignored the look. He was used to his father's disapproval.

The duke made of show of reading through some papers, ignoring the men in front of him. Luke waited, silent and unmoving. He would not allow either father to rile him.

Finally the duke looked up. "I must confess that this was not the conversation I expected to be having."

One of Luke's eyebrows drifted up. "I am afraid I don't understand."

"I thought you might give my daughter only a cursory amount of attention. Feign interest for the sake of your father's wishes." The duke paused to give him a level stare.

"I feign nothing," he replied evenly. The man needed to have more faith in his daughter's charms.

"Yes, I am aware." The older man cleared his throat. "Your interest was evident to every person present. What I am now concerned about is your intentions."

"My intentions are to marry her. Is that not why I am here?" He heard his father's intake of breath and he saw His Grace visibly relax. He relaxed as well, though he kept his body still, not wanting to reveal a thing.

"I am glad to hear it, as your interest bordered on scandalous." He cleared his throat. "As it stands, I think we should announce the engagement quickly."

"Nothing would make me happier than to agree." Luke leaned forward in his chair. "Lady Tabitha feels some hesitation do to my prior reputation—"

"I am also aware of my daughter's feelings," the duke cut in.

Luke's father cleared his throat but blessedly he remained quiet and allowed his son to continue on.

"I have told her that I would give her time so that I might prove myself."

"That is of little consequence—" the duke began.

"Your Grace," Luke interrupted, which was a risky maneuver. "With all due respect, you are married. How would your wife feel about you making promises to her that you did not keep? You well know how intelligent she is—"

"'Tis a plague, really." The duke looked up to the ceiling.

Luke relaxed, grinning. He had found the argument that would persuade the man to give him more time. If only he had been so effective with the daughter. "I can't speak to that. But Tabitha is unlikely to forget if I fail in my first promise, and I would see her happy in our marriage."

Tabbie's father assessed him for several seconds longer than was necessary but a small smile pulled at one corner of his lips. "Very good. I too would prefer to see my daughter happy and so I will grant you time. But keep your public attentions appropriate. We will be attending the Wilkinson's masquerade ball this coming Friday. You will join us." His eyes travelled over the earl, the hard edge returning. "Tricia is coming out this season. I'd like Tabbie engaged. If not to you then..." the duke allowed his words to trail off.

Luke tightened and he suppressed the rumble in his chest. Tabbie would be his, no one else's. But he wouldn't say that out loud now. The man who started the Wicked Earls' Club, the Earl of Coventry, had taught him a great deal about when to speak and when to remain quiet.

These skills had allowed him to substantially grow his holdings through successful negotiation. And he would use every skill he had to make Tabbie his.

He stood, shaking the duke's hand and exiting the man's study. It was absurd that two days prior he hadn't known her and that three days ago he'd been sure he would never marry.

Meeting her had shifted his focus in ways he hadn't thought possible. Hell, he had barely had a drink, hadn't thought about gambling, wanted nothing to do with light skirts, or any other woman for that matter. His life had come into sharp focus. This was the person he wanted to be.

His father, just behind him, reached out his hand. "Luke."

Luke slowed his pace to allow his father to catch up. He wasn't sure he wanted to discuss this now. "I must find Lady Tabitha and say my goodbyes before we return to London."

"You're truly serious about this lady?" His father raised his eyebrows.

Luke shrugged. "I am."

"May I ask, why her? I'm thrilled. It's what your mother and I have always wanted. I just expected it to be more difficult."

"I'll explain as soon as I can form it into the appropriate words. It isn't just that she is what I have wanted, it's that she brings out pieces of me that I thought gone."

His father's eye lit with surprise. "Coventry was right."

But Luke's own eyes narrowed. "What?"

"I don't know how the two of you are acquainted but he seems to know you well enough to suggest that the duke's daughter was an ideal match for you."

Coventry had been involved? He needed to get back to the club and speak with his mentor.

But first, he needed to find Tabbie.

* * *

TABBIE SAT STARING out the window as her mother droned on. "How long were you hiding behind that plant? It's ridiculous. You should have danced the night away. You're quite pretty, Tabbie. If only…" Her mother continued on but Tabbie ignored her.

Her mother had been so busy, she hadn't even noticed that Tabbie had snuck off to the library, nor had her mother realized that Luke had joined her behind said plant. Not that she intended to enlighten her mother, but really.

Nor was her mother aware that Tabbie wasn't listening. At least until her mother mentioned Luke. "I suppose you've managed to capture the attention of the Earl of Sussex, though his interest is almost upsetting. Such intensity. Perhaps I should speak to your father. Sussex leaves today and these sorts of visits often end without a contract. It wouldn't be unusual—"

Tabbie stood, interrupting her mother. This was her opportunity. If she and her mother rejected Luke's suit then her father would surely crumble. "If not Sussex, then who?"

Her mother blinked up at her. "Lord Crummell, of course." Her mother gave her a gentle smile. "He's rather smitten with you and unlike Sussex, he is a kind and personable man."

This should be excellent news, but the corners of her mouth turned down. Thoughts of marrying Crummell filled her with… dull dread. While he did seem perfectly nice, he was boring, not all that sharp, and not particularly manly. He'd never understand her the way Luke did. Nor would Crummell inspire the same feelings. If he kissed the way he danced, then her life would be passionless.

But was that better than the alternative? Luke was exciting, intelligent, and exhilarating, but likely to break her heart.

Her mother blinked at her again, clearly expecting some sort of response. "Forgive me, Mama. I need to think all of this over. Can we discuss this again later?"

Her mother gave her a genuine smile. "An excellent idea. A lady should take her time with such decisions. I'm glad to see you exercising some feminine restraint."

Her eyes nearly bulged out of her head at the words. Restraint was the last thing she practiced when with Luke. But with a nod, she swept out of her mother's room.

She needed quiet to sift through her swirling thoughts. She made her way to her own suite of rooms. Entering quickly, she locked the door behind her, not wishing to be disturbed.

Her breathing was ragged as she leaned her forehead against the wood door. Luke frightened her but Crummell might just frighten her more. Not in the same way. She'd likely be bored to death.

"What's wrong?" a deep rich voice spoke from just behind her.

She jumped and made to scream, but a hand covered her mouth, another snaking around her waist. The solid mass of a man pressing against her back. His touch was gentle and she heard him chuckle. Of course it was Luke's voice. Who else would think to enter her room uninvited? Her hands came up to his to move them away from her mouth. "What are you doing in here?"

"I needed to speak with you before I return to London," he rasped as his hand brushed down her neck to rest on her collarbone.

Her nerves jumped for an entirely different reason. He'd be in London, alone, with all those beautiful ladies. "If you get caught in here, there is no escaping the marriage noose."

"I thought I made it clear that I didn't want to escape."

"And I thought I made it clear that I was still deciding and you made it clear that you would allow me to do so." Irritation bubbled inside her and she turned in his arms to tell him just that.

But looking at him made productive conversation so difficult. Especially when Luke dipped his head to capture her lips. She was breathless by the time he lifted it again. "No one will find us, love. I promise."

"What are you doing here?" she repeated.

"I thought I told you already." One of his eyebrows shifted up as he brushed his thumb across her puffy lips.

"Obviously, I found your answer insufficient," she attempted to huff, but it came out breathy.

He searched her eyes, his own soft. "Since trust seems to be our biggest obstacle, I feared you would worry over our separation. I wanted to assure you, privately, that there is no need to fret. I will not so much as look at another woman until I see you on Friday."

She took a breath. Much as she appreciated his words, they did little to quell her real fears and her questions tumbled out. "What is happening Friday? What about after Friday? How would I even know you kept your promise?"

His lips covered hers in a breathless kiss that made her forget the rest of the questions bubbling inside which was likely his intent. Then he slowly raised his head. "Friday is the masquerade ball. You will be in attendance and I will make sure to be as well. Only you can decide if you can trust me this week and the weeks that follow. But I swear to you, Tabbie, if you choose to be my wife, there will be no other."

Tears pricked at her eyes as she looked up at him. She wanted to believe him, more than anything. But the seed of doubt that had been planted would not wash away. "I want to believe…" she whispered.

He kissed her a third time, pressing her back to the door. Then his lips began blazing a trail down her neck, over her collarbone.

She was so focused on the feel of his lips that she nearly missed his hands bunching up her skirts so that they rose above her knees to her thighs.

His voice was gruff as he kissed the valley between her breasts. "Let me show you what else I can give you." And then he dropped to his knees, his head disappearing under layers of fabric.

"What…what…are you…doing?" she gasped. But his fingers had parted her pantaloons, and slipping them in the slit of the fabric, he brushed her folds. Her hips jerked and her knees started to buckle but he used his broad shoulders to prop her up. Stroking her more deeply, she felt him open her up as his tongue touched her most intimate place.

She lost the ability to think or reason as the pleasure built inside her. His tongue caressed her over and over until she bit the inside of her cheek to keep from screaming out. Her legs refused to support her entirely as she trembled and clenched with the need building inside.

When he inserted a finger, deep into her channel, her pleasure broke apart, sending her body spasming into ecstasy.

Her body continued to shudder as he slowly withdrew his hand and pulled his head out from under her skirts. Then he swept her into his arms and carried her over to the bed.

Her head lay limply on his shoulder. "I didn't know," was all she could murmur.

She felt him smile as he pressed his lips to the top of her head. "I could give you that pleasure every night, love."

"And when you're gone?" she asked, lazily looking up at him.

"Why would I need to be gone?" He grinned. "We'll move to the country. Hire a staff that is all over the age of fifty."

They had reached the bed and she couldn't help but giggle as he gently laid her down. "This is ludicrous. You know that, don't you? *You* are trying to convince *me* to wed."

"Don't forget me this week," he kissed her tenderly on the lips. "I will see you on Friday."

The masquerade ball was on Friday. But her family would be travelling to London on Wednesday in preparation for the season. She didn't tell him that, though, because a plan was forming in her mind. A scheme, her mother would call it. Spying was most decidedly a scheme.

CHAPTER 6

The week passed dreadfully slowly. While his body felt amazing, his mind sharp without the entrapment of liquor, he missed Tabbie.

She had tasted sweeter than any woman he'd ever known, and bloody hell, she'd been so tight around his finger.

And her reaction. Hells bells, she was wanton as her unruly curls had suggested, wet and willing and so damn beautiful.

Even more amazing was that his feelings went far deeper than that. It was her wit and her kindness that made him long for her company. He dreamed about her at night, thoughts of her hardly left his mind throughout the day. She had stolen, not just his affection, but apparently his every thought.

He had to chuckle. A pretty little wallflower was the undoing of a rake.

It hadn't helped that Coventry had been travelling and Luke wouldn't be able to speak to him until Thursday. He wanted to know what part the other man had played in Tabbie entering his life.

Finally, he received a missive from Coventry to join him at the club that evening. Luke grimaced. He would miss the club, at least his friends within. He would still see them of course, but he promised Tabbie a life in the country and he would deliver. Besides, he looked forward to that life. He wasn't sure when it had happened but at some point, he'd grown tired of the lifestyle. It had taken Tabbie to make him see what he should have realized earlier. But this life of full wakefulness was so much more fulfilling.

Having risen early, he'd already been to his boxing club, worked on his accounting books, gone riding in the park. As the afternoon wore on, he finally decided to make his way toward Asher Street. He'd walk to the club in a roundabout path that would alleviate some of his nervous energy.

He wasn't worried about the meeting with Coventry or about the masquerade ball. In fact, he was eager for both events. But a dread was building in his chest that he didn't quite understand. Attempting to suss out his feelings, he picked up the pace as he rounded a nearby park when he heard what sounded like a feminine huff of breath.

Stopping, he turned to look but saw nothing. Perhaps it had been a bird? He continued walking but his pace was slower and then he stopped to examine some flowers that were peeking out of the ground. Glancing back, he saw nothing, but as he started walking again, the distinct sound of silk skirts rustling caught his ears. Was a woman following him?

He rounded the corner to the club and made his way up Asher Street. It must be one of the ladies who worked within the club. He had simply looked the wrong way and didn't see her, had missed her passing. Or perhaps it was a lady who lived further down Asher Street. No well-heeled lady would be foolish enough to travel this far out of London proper.

With a shrug, he inserted his key into the lock and stepped inside. As he closed the door, he caught sight of a hooded woman. It wasn't terribly cold, spring had warmed the air, so it was curious that she had pulled the hood up. A single auburn curl floated in the breeze, but she tucked it back and ducked her head lower.

His eyes scrunched together as he made his way down the hall. The cloak had looked to be made of a fine wool, which was odd for this neighborhood. Perhaps it was one of the maids from the club. They often had admirers among the earls who bought them fancy gifts. But she would have come to the back entrance. He continued to puzzle over it as he veered right, toward Coventry's private office within the building.

He knocked and Coventry called, "Come in."

Opening the door, his mind still grappled with the lady in the cloak. "Thanks for seeing me."

"Of course. How did you fare with Lady Tabitha?"

"You know very well how I fared." Luke raised an eyebrow.

"You always were a smart one." Coventry nodded as he gave a benign smile. "Did she scheme her way into your heart?"

So he knew about Tabbie's tendency for plotting did he? A thousand questions rushed to his mind. How did Coventry know her? How had he known that they would be well matched? "Actually she tried to scheme her way out of our engagement."

Coventry's eyes lit with appreciation and interest as he leaned forward in his chair. "Clever girl, pushing you away. What was her plan?"

"How do you even know that she would have a plan?" Luke leaned forward too. Coventry was like family to him, but it was odd that the man knew so much about Tabbie. And yet, he had never spoken of her.

Coventry sat back then. "When she managed to open her shelter, despite a great deal of dissent from a fair number of lords, I knew she would make an excellent match for one of my errant earls. The question was which one. Which man would like a girl with spirit and brains, and fiery auburn hair to match her vivacious approach to life?"

His friend, and leader of the Wicked Earls' Club, was a matchmaker? Luke couldn't process the words because another detail had clicked in his mind. His little schemer with her fiery auburn hair. She wouldn't have made a wild plan to follow him, say to the Wicked Earls' Club to see what he was doing?

Fear made his heart stutter as he stood from his chair, knocking the heavy piece of furniture to the ground. "Grab some men and pistols," he nearly shouted as he shot back out the door and down the hall.

* * *

BLAST... Luke had disappeared behind a locked door. She'd heard the bolt click back into place. She followed him for near a mile, her feet were positively aching. And it was for naught. Anything could be behind that door.

"Tabbie, I think we should go home." Tricia's voice shook as she finally caught up wither sister. She wasn't as adept at subterfuge and had lagged behind so as not to give them away. "Mother thinks we are shopping for ribbon and I don't think this the best place for us—"

"Give me a moment," Tabbie shushed her sister. "There must be a way inside."

"We can't go inside," Tricia hissed.

Tabbie patted her on the arm. "Not you, just me. You can act as lookout." Glancing down the street, she noticed an alley between this building and the next. "Maybe there is a back way in."

Standing, she shook out her skirts and stepped down onto the sidewalk. Tricia sat on the steps, looking forlornly toward the park from where they had come. Clearly her sister wanted to return.

Tabbie was about to chastise her sister's sense of adventure when she noticed three men across the street silently assessing her. Perhaps she had dismissed Tricia too easily.

Their clothes were worn, faces unshaved, hats pulled low. Nothing about them spoke of respectability or even decency.

The corner of her mouth pulled down into a frown. She'd come all this way, she hated to give up now, but it didn't seem like the best idea to traipse down a dark alley with ruffians looking on. "Or perhaps we should come back another time."

"Thank the saints," Tricia exhaled, giving her a large smile. Tabbie's eyes flitted over Tricia. At sixteen she was growing into a lovely woman, who was a great deal more demure than her older sister. Tricia would find husband hunting quite easy. But in a situation like this, Tricia was at more risk. She didn't have a sharp tongue and bravado to fall back on. Tabbie shouldn't have brought her here.

Movement from the men on the other side of the street caught her eye as they began crossing toward them. For a split second she wondered what to do. Pound on the door behind her or make a hasty retreat the way she had come. Their eyes locked on her, they were closing the distance between them quickly.

"Bang on the door," Tabbie hissed to Tricia.

"We can't do that, we followed him--" Tricia started but she stopped as she turned and caught sight of the ruffians. Gathering up her skirts, Tricia raced up the stairs and started banging on the door.

Tabbie squared her shoulders, not sure how she would defend her sister against these men, but she knew she had to try.

"Well aren't you a pretty little thing." One of the men leered at her as they all approached. He was tall and thin, his clothing stained.

Her skin crawled but she lifted her chin. "I can assure you, sir, my friend will be joining us momentarily." She forced her voice to be steady despite the fear building within her chest.

Another cackled. Her shoulders drooped just a little but she squared them back up. Tricia was still pounding on the door.

"Of course 'e is," another called. "But in the meantime, you ladies can take off yer jewels and yer reticules."

The leering one let his eyes wander down her. "And mayhap we'll continue this conversation more private, like in the alley."

Tabbie couldn't help herself, she stepped back then. Her heels bumping into the wrought iron fence edging the beds in the front of the building. "Never," she tried to say with confidence but it came out as a whisper. Her fingers came to the base of her neck. This wasn't going to end well.

The leering one grabbed her arm while another attempted to wrest her reticule from her clenched fist.

"Grab the other one," the man yanking on her arm commanded as he gave her a firm tug.

"No," she gasped, pulling back, still holding tight to her reticule.

He leaned in, his breath as foul as the stains on his shirt. His lips curling into a malicious smile that made her more afraid than when he'd grabbed her. "Oh, we'll have ye bo—"

His words stopped abruptly as a fist bashed into his teeth. Suddenly she was spinning around a large body, firm hands lifting her in the air. She landed on the stairs, still standing, as Luke threw two more punches, knocking another man to the ground.

Tabbie blinked, trying to understand her sudden change in fortune when the man who had been attempting to pull away her reticule, pulled a knife from her waist and waved it at Luke. "That's enough of that." He gave Luke a hard eye.

"I disagree," a man spoke behind her, his voice as hard as stone that had both her and Tricia jumping in the air before they turned. New fear trickled down Tabbie's back. Who else had joined this menagerie?

He gave a curt nod, to acknowledge her. An elderly looking man, impeccably dressed, he stepped next to her, holding out two pistols. She recognized the Earl of Coventry immediately. "I've sent a man to collect The Bow Street Runners. You may as well have a seat, gentlemen."

Two other men came out the door, Lord Gracon and another. For the first time since this began, a blush heated her cheeks. She'd be ruined for this. As if reading her thoughts, the elderly gentleman turned to Luke. "Take the ladies home. We'll not speak of this to anyone."

Grabbing her arm, Luke guided her and Tricia to the now infamous alley where a carriage sat unattended. Luke opened the door and she and her sister climbed in. "Where did you leave your carriage?"

"The ribbon shop on Regent Street," she croaked, her voice cracking.

He gave a curt nod and then made to climb in the driver's seat.

"Luke?" Her voice was desperate, she knew it. She'd made a terrible mistake and she'd have to answer for it.

He gave her a hard look, his usual soft demeanor gone. "What, Tabbie?"

He'd used her given name at least. "I'm so sorry."

His face softened and he pulled her against his chest, his cheek pressed against her hair. "You frightened me."

"I know. It was a foolish, silly thing to do."

"We'll talk about it later. Right now, let's get you home." And then he pulled away and handed her into the carriage. She missed his heat. More than anything she wanted to press close to him where it was warm and safe.

Tricia sat in the seat across from her, eyes as wide as saucers. "He saved us."

"I am so sorry I put you in that situation." Tabbie looked at her sister who then launched herself across the carriage and into her arms.

"It's all right. I understand. I know you are trying to figure out if he is the right man for you, but after all of that, don't you think you'll marry him?"

She took a breath, after what she'd put her sister through, she owed Tricia as much of the truth as a sixteen-year-old could hear. "Part of me wants to. He is so handsome and brave. When he looks at me, it is like the sun shining upon me." Tabbie took a breath. "But I am afraid, after I give myself to him, he will grow tired of this little wallflower, and turn his sights elsewhere."

Her sister patted her arm. "I know you are afraid. But you won't know for sure until you give yourself to him."

She blinked three times. "What?"

"You have to give him your heart to know if he'll take it and keep it close to his." Tricia smiled up at her.

Tabbie nodded. For a moment, she thought her sister had been advising her to give Luke her chastity. The trouble with just handing over her heart was that they would be married by the time she would understand if he truly meant to keep it.

But if she gave him her innocence... Well, she'd have a chance to see if, after they were intimate, he turned his eye to another woman.

Her leg twitched under her gown. It was so risky. If discovered, they'd be married. Her father wouldn't allow her to be ruined.

She pushed down the voice of dissent that told her she was using this as an excuse to be with him without waiting for marriage. He did make her feel things no other man had.

But wouldn't it be better to know if he'd move on to another woman before she tied herself to him forever?

CHAPTER 7

Nerves fluttered in her belly as she made her way toward the dance floor. Her trembling hand reached up to adjust the domino mask on her face for the hundredth time in the last half hour.

Luke was late. But rather than irritation, a small smile touched her lips. It was a trait she found endearing rather than annoying, a little window into who he was. A man who rarely followed social convention.

But all the same, she hated these events and it would be so much more bearable by his side…in his arms.

A hand brushed her back and she turned smiling broadly, expecting to see Luke, but it wasn't him. The Marquess of Crummell stood appraising her. "My lady," he grinned back, not realizing it wasn't a smile meant for him. "I must confess, your greeting fills my heart with joy."

She bit back a sigh. She couldn't very well tell him that it hadn't been meant for him. "I'm glad, my lord." She took a half step away. "If you will excuse me."

He reached for her hand. "I'd like to ask for a dance, if I may."

With a tight smile, she offered her card to him and he placed his name in not one, but two places.

Drat. It would limit her time with Luke. Her opportunity to sneak away with him and allow him...

Her thoughts ended because he was there, behind her. She felt rather than saw him, but she knew it was Luke by the way her body tightened, filling with a tension she couldn't name.

His warm breath blew across her exposed neck. Goosebumps rose on her arms and she longed to melt back against him. But it simply wasn't proper. Not that what she planned was proper.

Without a word, he took her dance card and wrote his name for three dances, all in a row. Crummell spluttered. It was scandalous. Without a formal commitment, it wasn't done.

As Crummell had placed himself for the next set, he offered her his elbow. "Might I sit with you while we wait?"

Her eyes darted to Luke. He watched her with unwavering attention, his dark eyes smoldering. She had so much to say to him. The longer she'd thought about the events from the day before, the more she wanted to throw herself into his arms. He'd saved her and her sister. She wanted to apologize for being such a fool, kiss every inch of his face as a thank you, and then beg him to touch her...everywhere. Merciful heaven, she was supposed to be testing his resolve. Would he make love to her and then leave her? She wasn't sure it mattered. He had her heart now. Even if he rejected her, would she want to take it back?

She started at the realization and her eyes widened. She was in love with him.

He moved closer, blocking Crummell. "Answer the man. He asked to sit with you." The intensity was still heating his gaze but a small smile played at his lips.

"Oh, I apologize. I was distracted and I..." Her voice trailed off. What was she to say? *I was distracted by the heated gaze of the other man we are talking to? I only just realized that I more than lust after him? I am, in fact, in love with him?*

"She doesn't want to sit with you, Crummell." Luke's eyes never left hers.

Crummell straightened. She only knew it was true because the top of his head peeked over Luke's shoulder. "I will report your behavior to her father, sir. Indecent. You will have to answer for it and—"

"She is to be my wife." Luke turned to face the other man but she caught his gaze hardening before he did. "Don't bother collecting your dances."

"That is absurd." Crummell spluttered but she saw him shrink back down. "The duke shall most certainly hear about this."

Tabbie suppressed a grin. She would have liked to have told Crummell to be gone but a woman couldn't be so openly confrontational. Crummell stormed off and she moved closer to Luke, her cheek just brushing his sleeve.

He turned back to her, his expression soft. "We need to discuss a few things."

Her insides flipped and her shoulders hunched. "We do," she murmured.

THEY BEGAN SKIRTING THE CROWD, moving to a more private location. It took several minutes and fear built inside of her as she trailed behind him. Once the space opened up, he stopped moving and twisted his elbow toward her so that she might slip her hand through it. The feel of his heat and strength through his clothes calmed her fears.

What was she afraid of? He'd just declared they would marry. Was she afraid of losing her maidenhead? No, the prospect filled her with excitement. Her feelings? With every passing moment, she grew less concerned that he would hurt her emotionally, though it still nagged at her.

She would still follow through with her plan. Because it was sound. It really did give her the opportunity to discover if her future husband would lose interest after intimacy. The fact that she wouldn't have to wait for his touch was an added benefit.

So what was making her tremble so? Then she knew. If her father found out about any of this, he'd lock her in a tower until she was too old to marry at all.

"What are you thinking?" Luke's eyes were searching her face as they moved closer to the terrace doors.

So much swirled in her head, she didn't quite know where to begin. "Yesterday, I was so foolish."

But he only winked as he swept her though the doors, mindless of the complete lack of decorum in taking her outside unchaperoned. At least the space was filled with other partygoers. "Tabbie, it is not the last time I will have to untangle you from some scrape you have landed yourself in, I suspect. It's part of what makes you interesting."

"I don't mean to cause such trouble." She bit her lip as she assessed his profile next to her.

"But somehow, you always do." It wasn't his voice that answered, it was her father's. He'd snuck up next to them without her even realizing.

A tremble shook through her. It wasn't that her father was a villain, or even mean spirited. It was that he held her future in his grasp and she was near powerless to redirect him. As a duke, he expected to be obeyed.

"Papa." She unhooked her hand from Luke's arm and turned toward her father. Dread made her quake. Luke turned too, and grasping her other hand, tucked that into his elbow. The gesture was not lost on her father. His eyes narrowed as he assessed Luke. "I told you to act with decorum."

"The terrace is sufficiently chaperoned," Luke answered quietly.

"You refused to allow another man to dance with her," her father fired back.

Luke's own eyes narrowed before he responded. "He intends to win her affection."

Her father sighed deeply. "And how likely is that without my intervention?"

"Do you intend to intervene?" Luke tensed underneath her hand.

Her father took a step closer. "He's a marquess."

Luke shrugged at that. "I will be as well."

Her mind, a jumble of thoughts suddenly sharpened. Her father was considering Crummell. What he needed was a reason not to consider the other man, to favor Luke. The issue of title fell in Crummell's favor but it occurred to her that if her father thought Luke had ruined her, he'd have no choice but to wed her and Luke and dismiss Crummell forever.

"You deliberately disobeyed me—" His eyes bore into Luke.

"Papa," she interrupted. "We have feelings—"

"Don't be foolish." Her father's lip curled. "One would think your intelligence endowed you with a bit more sense."

All the dread she had been feeling bloomed into white-hot anger. Her father never gave her credit. He always expected her to act as her mother did, but she wasn't like her mother. "You are correct. I am a terrible fool who allowed a known rake to court her. Oh wait…that was you." Her hand tightened around Luke's elbow.

"Tabbie, you will keep your tongue sweet and you will obey me."

"It's too late, Papa. I've allowed Luke to—"

"Tabbie—" It was Luke's strong voice that stopped her words. "Crummell is waiting for his dance."

She blinked in complete confusion. He turned to look at her and gave her a tiny wink on the side that her father couldn't see. It was all the assurance she needed and with a nod, she left his side, stepped around her father and headed back toward the music.

Above all odds, she trusted Luke with her heart and with her future.

* * *

LUKE STARED at the man in front of him. It was time to make Tabbie his and stop allowing her father to have control.

"How did you manage to have Tabbie obey you so easily?" His Grace's eyes followed his daughter through the doors.

"She knows that I only want what is best for her." Luke's arms crossed in silent accusation.

"Are your public displays of impropriety best for her? I am considering Lord Crummell just to save her reputation."

"You are considering Lord Crummell so that you may continue to exercise control over the both of them." Luke's hands clenched into fists against his chest.

The other man's face tightened. "Are you trying to sway me toward him? That is a most excellent argument. Now what was Tabbie about to say?"

Luke felt a muscle tick in his jaw. He had to proceed very carefully. "She was being Tabbie. Impulsive and likely to say whatever she thought would result in our marriage."

His Grace stepped closer. "Or you are a rogue who has compromised my daughter."

Luke assessed the man in front of him. "I have done as you have asked."

He gave a nod. "Excellent." His grace gave him a cold smile. "Then there is still time to consider other suitors."

Another man might have begged, groveled, or even thrown a fist. But Luke was not any of those men. Instead he gave his grace a small salute. "Do as you see fit." Then he followed Tabbie back into the ball.

Because a scheme was exactly what this situation required.

His world seemed to slow as he watched Crummell attempt to

spin her around on the polished marble floor. That man didn't deserve a woman like Tabbie. It was laughable.

As the set came to an end, he intercepted them on the way to return Tabbie to her mother. He didn't say a word as he held out his arm to her and she slipped her gloved hand into the crook of his elbow.

They took a position on the floor and then began to effortlessly glide as the strains of a waltz filled the room.

"How did it go with my father?" she asked as his hand clutched at her waist.

He gave a shake of his head and then told her about the conversation that had transpired. "I promised you time to decide, my love. I am sorry to take it from you now."

"You are not, my father is." Her eyes glowed up at him, shining in the dim light. His moon goddess, looking even more mysterious in her mask.

He wished he could kiss her. Instead, he asked, "Have you decided if you prefer my suit or that of another?"

Her body brushed against his. "You are my choice. My heart is yours."

Hellfire and damnation, he wanted to sweep her from this room and kiss her until they'd both gone blind from it. But instead he pressed his lips to her ear. "Then we must form a plan."

CHAPTER 8

While Tabbie had tried to convince Luke to simply ruin her, in the end, they had decided to elope. It had a certain poetic beauty, as far as schemes went, and he could ruin her thoroughly during the journey to Gretna Green.

The part that was rather startling was that it was decided to leave that very night. So here she sat on her bed in her riding cloak and sturdy travel clothes, a bag of necessaries and trinkets at half past two in the morning.

Which was the time he was supposed to arrive, but she settled in to wait. Luke would likely be late.

Surprise rippled through her as her window cracked open and his head appeared. With strong arms, he pulled himself through the opening and landed with a soft thud on the carpet.

"You're on time," she giggled, surprised.

He quirked an eyebrow. "Are you saying I am normally late?"

"Always." Standing, she crossed the room and wrapped her arms around his waist. "We are truly eloping?"

He gave a nod and then captured her lips with his. "I simply can't sleep another night without my moon goddess." His lips captured hers again. "Besides, this gives us the element of surprise. If we wait, your father will have time to grow suspicious."

She gave a nod, her entire body tingling with excitement and desire. She loved a good scheme and somehow it only seemed to amplify her passion for Luke. "Will we climb back out the window?"

"And risk breaking that pretty neck?" He trailed kisses down its column. "No, I have a carriage waiting one alley over. We'll walk out the back door."

She rolled her eyes in mock protest. "How dull."

"I could put you in breeches and then you could climb out. I think I should like to see that." His husky whisper only made her shiver with want.

"Let's go. Before we are caught." She tugged on his hand, toward her bedroom door.

He softly pulled on the handle but the door refused to move. Turning back to her, both his eyebrows moved toward his hairline. "Apparently, your father is suspicious already."

Tabbie's lips twisted into a frown. She should have known her father would be suspicious but it was still irritating. "What do we do now?"

But rather than answer, Luke picked her up and slung her easily over his shoulder. "Stay still and close your eyes." And then he was crossing the room toward the window.

"Luke," she gasped clutching the back of his shirt. "You're not actually going to—" But she stopped as he began climbing out the window. One look at the ground from her second story vantage point, perched upside down on Luke's shoulder, and she did as he said and squeezed her eyes shut as her breath came out in ragged huffs.

He made quick work of the trellis and landed them both on the ground. "Don't move," he ordered as he scaled back up the trellis and then reappeared with her travel bag.

Shaking her head, she huffed when he landed next to her. "You are trying to kill me."

Pulling her close, he captured her lips again, making her breathless for an entirely different reason. As he slowly pulled back his lips, he touched his nose to hers. "You were the one who said going out the door was dull."

Chuckling, her insides glowed with happiness, as he pulled her down the street and to the alley. "Were you able to secure passage?" she whispered in the quiet night.

"Yes, on a lovely ship. I think you were correct, that is the better way to travel. Your father will immediately begin checking all the popular post and stage coach stations."

Her insides fluttered, not from excitement but fear. "My father may very well disown me. I'll likely have no dowry."

"It doesn't bother me if it's all right with you." He kissed her long and slow.

Nodding, she rested her forehead against his. "It's strange to cut ties with your family. I am putting my life completely in your hands, Luke."

His fingers laced with hers. "I know you've had your reservations; I can't tell you how much your trust in me means. I love you, Tabbie. I'll never hurt you."

"Thank you," her voice was scratchy as though she were holding back tears. She wasn't, she told herself as she swiped at a small drop of water on her cheek. "I love you, too."

"When we return, I will set up an account of money for you. If for any reason you are dissatisfied, you could live comfortably on your own. I know it doesn't replace your family, but it gives you some measure of independence."

Her heart nearly stopped in her chest. She would never have asked for such a gift. While her heart still ached over the loss of her family, it was so much easier to trust knowing that he had provided her with an alternate option. "Oh Luke," her words failed and so she used her lips to express her feeling by pressing them to his.

The kiss deepened, lengthened until her head was so muddled she could think of nothing else but him. Their bodies were pressed together and without even realizing it was happening, she found herself sitting sideways on his lap, her derriere cradled between his legs, the hard press of him against her soft flesh.

"Luke," she gasped, wanting more, wanting all of him.

He didn't answer as the carriage came to an abrupt halt. Paying the driver, he handed her out of the buggy and holding her hand, they walked down the docks toward a cluster of ships.

A large vessel stood apart and she grinned as Luke propelled them toward it. *The Destiny* emblazoned on her side. "You didn't pick this ship for the name, did you?"

He gave her a wink. "I ship a decent amount of cargo to Scotland. I work with the captain often."

They made their way up the plank and then were ushered into the captain's quarters where a buffet of food was already laid out for them.

She turned to Luke. "What's all this?"

"I told them we were recently wed and going to visit your family in Scotland." Luke popped a fig in his mouth, as his eyes devoured her.

She blushed to her roots. "How long will the journey take?" Some of her desire had cooled, replaced with little niggles of fear. She'd already traveled past any redemption with her family and perhaps with society, but here, alone with him, this felt like the moment that would change everything.

His eyes never left hers as he reached for her and pulled her closer. "Three or four days. Similar to the land journey and hopefully less taxing."

"Where will we go after the wedding?" She swallowed the lump in her throat.

His lips brushed her temple. "To my country estate in Norfolk, though I haven't been there in some time. It may be a bit…rustic at first. It will have to be staffed and—"

"I'm sure it will be fine." Nerves gripped at her belly. "We can return to London if you'd prefer. I—" But the idea of returning to London made her heart beat wildly.

"No, my love," he whispered close to her ear. His arms wrapped around her, holding her tightly. The fear that had been building was replaced with an emotion of another kind entirely… desire. She recognized it now. "We will spend some time just the two of us. Build trust," he murmured as his lips brushed her cheek. "Which leads me to my next point. It will be difficult, since we are sharing a room, but I want to wait to be intimate until after we are married."

Her stomach near dropped to the floor as her head reared back. "What?"

He gave a low chuckle. "It sounds awful, I know. But this is a fresh start for me and I want to do it correctly."

She gave him a sideways glance, a small smile playing at her lips. He was protecting her, giving her the very best of himself and she appreciated it more than she could possibly say. But her fear was gone, and in its wake, was a rising need to be close to him. "Am I the only woman you won't practice your roguish charm on?"

It was his turn to look stunned. Then, with a flurry of ribbons and fabric, her cloak was off and the buttons of her dress undone. "Just because I won't take your maidenhead, does not mean I can't act like a rogue."

As her dress slipped off her shoulders, his lips followed a trail behind them. When he reached the top of her chemise, his fingers came to the ties of her corset and in moments, the boned piece fell away. Dimly, she thought her personal maid would be jealous of the dexterity with which he removed the pieces.

But all thought left her as his hands came to her breasts, cupping them, his thumb brushing her nipples. "Oh," she gasped as his mouth dropped to suck on the flesh still covered by the chemise.

The chemise sailed over her head and he made quick work of the rest of her clothing. She wasn't even aware they were moving until her legs brushed the back of the bed. Shrugging off his own jacket and shirt, he lay her down. His lips once again kissing a trail across her body that left her blazing with heat. She whimpered and writhed, her body wanting more of him touching her, more contact within, deeper and stronger.

His fingers grasped her hips and then one of them floated to her inner thigh, reaching up and brushing her folds. Her hips bucked as his mouth continued to kiss lower.

Digging her fingers into his broad hard shoulders, she tried to think, attempted to reason out why they might not be as intimate as they could possibly be when his lips kissed between the juncture of her legs. A moan escaped her and her fingers dug into his hair as he brought her pleasure higher, until she could barely stand another moment and then it broke. She cried his name, her body twisting against him.

One of his hands still held her hip and he pressed kisses along her thigh. His voice was hoarse as he muttered. "Is that better, my love?"

"Mmmh," she murmured. Her eyes drifting closed. The sun was just beginning to rise and she stroked his hair. "So good."

He kissed his way back up her body as he chuckled. She sank into the mattress, a vision of being tucked into his side as they slept together. "I'm glad."

As he moved to pepper her chest with kisses, she felt the hard press of his manhood against her leg. That was when she realized, she had found release but he hadn't. He wasn't denying her pleasure, only himself. Why? Was he afraid? Worried his feelings would change once they had been intimate?

But she didn't ask. Talking was for later.

His lips had reached the sensitive flesh of her ear and as he suckled it, he slid his body off to the side, taking her with him as he rolled, pressing her against him.

"I've dreamed of sleeping next to you," he whispered.

Her hand came to his bare chest, and then it drifted lower. "You did?" She kissed one of the hard ridges along his abdomen. She pushed those feeling of inadequacy away. She wouldn't do this out of fear, only love. She wanted to be close to him, to show him how she felt.

Then, ever so gently, she slipped her hand into his breeches. She didn't have to search far before velvety flesh met her fingertips.

His breath sucked in. "Tabbie," he hissed.

"Pleasure isn't just for me." She loved him. She wanted to give him everything that he had given to her.

"I can wait. I've spent my life indulging. Now is the time for me to prove that I can give and not receive. I want that for you, Tabbie. I want to be the type of man who deserves your love."

Her heart swelled with those words. "Love is best shared." She wrapped her hand around his member because she was curious, but his sudden intake of breath told her he liked it too. "Now show me how to share with you."

She watched his eyes narrow and dilate as he undid the laces of his breeches and pulled them down over his hips. His hand grasped hers and began a rhythmic movement that had them both panting with desire as their eyes locked. "Yes," he groaned as she moved up and down his smooth skin, her hand barely fitting around his member. She wasn't sure why, but the size of it excited her, left her more breathless, and before she thought about it, she slid down to place a kiss on its tip.

A moan ripped from his mouth, as his hand tangled in her hair. Sucking him deeper into her mouth, she relished the taste of him, the smell. The closeness it brought to pleasure him in this way.

His movements grew erratic as his breath heaved. And then he exploded, his seed filling her mouth. She wasn't sure what she had expected but as she licked and sucked, nothing had ever felt more right.

She would have continued to worship him but his hand suddenly grasped her under the arms and hauled her up his body. "What was that?"

She gave him a grin as she wrapped her arms around his neck. "I didn't know it would be like that, but it was glorious. Will it be like that when we're married?"

She felt him relax under her body and he tucked his head against her shoulder. "It will be even better."

THE JOURNEY to Gretna Green passed in languid bliss. They held each other, talked of the future, and of the past. Tabbie tried not to think of her family or what she left behind. Despite a strained relationship with her parents, she would miss them if they chose to cut her out of their lives. And her siblings? She loved them fiercely. Would they forgive her for leaving them?

She hadn't had a choice. Well, actually she did have a choice, and she had made it. She wouldn't look back now, but some of her old doubts continued creeping into her thoughts. The ones that worried Luke wouldn't remain interested or faithful. And then where would she be without a family or a real husband?

But she pushed these doubts aside as she made her way down the plank, or at least she tried to. It was too late to change anything. She'd made her choice.

Besides, even if it were possible to change it, she wasn't sure she could. She was hopelessly in love.

Luke found a hackney who took them directly to the nearest church. Though the ceremony could have been performed by a blacksmith, they'd decided to seek a church first. Somehow, Tabbie couldn't break from that tradition.

Her stomach flitted with butterflies as they stepped into the sun. "We're actually going to do this." Her voice shook more than she had intended.

Luke eyed her. "Nervous?" He reached his hand for hers and gave it a squeeze.

"Isn't every bride?" she gave him a bright smile, her lips stretched tight with the effort. "How are you?" Her voice was more genuine as she asked the question—concern for him not something she needed to hide, unlike her worries.

He stopped walking and gave her a gentle smile. "I am thrilled to be here, Tabbie. And you will share in my enthusiasm as soon as the ceremony is over. Let's find an inn where we can stay for tonight."

"And tomorrow?" She swallowed.

"We begin the journey to our new home."

Our home. The words warmed her. Strengthened her. She had been tempted to ask about the provision he'd said he would make for her future but it seemed as though she didn't trust him if she asked.

Staring out the window of the hackney, she knew the silence was building, but she couldn't bring herself to end it. Luke gave her a few glances but didn't break the silence either.

At some point these feelings would have to be addressed but their wedding day didn't seem the time. Or perhaps it was the most important time but everything would change once she did.

"Tell me about our home. You said it's in Norfolk?" She finally turned to him.

Luke breathed a sigh of relief. She heard it audibly rattle out of his chest. "Is that what you're concerned about?" He gave a little laugh and relaxed back into his seat. "The house is built in the curve of a river that leads out to the ocean. The gardens are stunning. Creeves has been the gardener there for thirty years. My father hired him before he took the title of marquess."

"What else?" She smiled a little. Hearing him speak helped to calm her nerves.

"We'll likely have to renovate. It's been years since anything has been updated. It will keep us busy for some time."

"Together?" she perked up.

"Of course. I couldn't do it without you. We may have to make a few trips to London to purchase materials, but we'll put it off for as long as we can."

"London…" Her voice trailed off, but the dread crept into it. The fears she didn't want to name had a place. *London.*

He heard it too. "We don't have to go. But I won't travel without you. If we do go, we'll do it together."

Tabbie closed her eyes. She wasn't being fair. He'd done nothing but reassure her and all she could do was allow doubts to creep in. "I'd like that." She gave him another, more genuine smile and scooted closer to him.

"Tabbie, tell me what is bothering you." He wrapped his arm around her shoulders and pulled her tight against his body.

"It isn't worth repeating," she replied softly.

"Repeating?" He raised an eyebrow and she softened at his charming expression.

"I've left my family." She swallowed hard. "My father isn't a forgiving man, which means I may never see them again."

Luke squeezed her close. "We'll have each other, my love. I won't leave you alone, I swear it."

* * *

A LUMP FORMED in Luke's throat as he stared at his bride, the words of the priest washing over him. He'd spent the last few days watching her become increasingly quiet but he'd been unsure what to do about it.

"Marriage is a promise to love, honor, and cherish…" The priest's lilting voice carried throughout the church despite the pews being empty.

Luke wondered if he was already failing at his promise.

Because the pews should be filled with her family. And his. But he hadn't wanted to take a chance that her father might rule in another man's favor and so he'd stolen her away. Like the rogue that he was.

"I do," Tabbie murmured.

With their hands tied together, Luke looked into her eyes. She didn't fully trust her heart to him yet, but she would in time. And he could help earn that trust by doing right by her, now. Not acting the part of rake but being an honorable man.

"You may kiss your bride," the priest said.

Luke pulled her close and captured her lips with his own. "I love you, Tabbie," he said as he kissed her again. He hadn't known before how to help her but now he knew what to do.

Her eyes shined back at him. "I love you, too."

Luke signed all the necessary documents and then grabbed a spare piece of parchment and penned a quick note. Once he was done, he returned to Tabbie and hand in hand, they walked back to the hired hack. He handed her in and then, stepping to the front, he handed the driver a note. "Once you've dropped us off at the inn, would you please deliver this to *The Destiny*."

"Aye, sir." The driver gave him a pleasant smile and then Luke joined his bride in the carriage intent upon telling her his plan.

The evening light was fading to dusk, decorating the interior of the hackney in a pink light. Her skin glowed and her smile was free and easy. He couldn't help himself. As he stepped in, he leaned over to kiss her.

Her lips were soft and so inviting beneath his. One kiss blended into another then a third until the hack jolted to a stop in front of the inn.

Sweeping her out of the carriage, they hurried to their room. His hand near trembled as he made to light a single candle. His moon goddess moved to the window. "Our wedding night," she murmured, her skin radiant in the semi-darkness of the room.

"Yes it is, my little moon goddess." A growl rumbled deep from in his chest. He felt predatory looking at her like that. The closeness without being inside her had been a delicious torture, but now it was about to come to an end.

He dropped his shirt from his shoulders before he even reached her and as his lips crashed down on hers, his hands expertly plucked the clothing from her body.

Once she was naked, he trailed his lips over her body. She tasted as sweet as she looked. It was strange, he'd never found a woman so pleasing to all of his senses. "I could taste you forever," he whispered against her belly.

Wrapping his fingers around her thigh, he pressed lightly between her legs. He heard her gasp then moan and he smiled as her legs started to give, unable to support her. Nudging her back till she rested against the wall, he let his mouth drift lower till he was spreading her legs, nudging her thigh onto his shoulder.

She loved the feel of his tongue, he knew she did, and he'd never grow tired of giving her what she loved. As her moans grew needier, he increased the pressure, sliding a finger inside of her.

She crashed around him and then wilted against the wall. "I thought tonight you made me your wife in full," she gasped as he picked her up and carried her to the bed.

"I intend to, my love." He kissed her even as he held her with one arm and removed his breeches with the other.

"Can women only enjoy a man's mouth?" she asked. He could feel the heat radiating from her cheeks. She was embarrassed by the question but he loved her innocence nearly as much as her enthusiasm for their bed sport.

"No, my love, they enjoy the act as well. Most of them, at least." He lay her down, taking in the sight of her naked, perfect round breasts accentuated by her tiny waist and flat belly and the flare of her hips. A patch of red hair pointed him exactly where he needed to be.

"Then why did we just do that?" Even in the dark he could see her blush as he climbed on top of her.

"It will soften you for the first time," he whispered. "I would not hurt you for anything."

"I trust you." She held her arms up to him and his chest swelled with love and pride to have earned this woman's trust.

Spreading her legs, he positioned himself at the opening. "Slow or quick?" he asked wanting to know how she'd prefer this be done.

"Do it quickly," she gasped and he could see her tense.

Leaning down, he placed his mouth over hers, kissing till she responded, softening in his arms and then he pushed himself inside of her.

Crying out, her arms grasped his biceps and he stilled, allowing her time to adjust. "Are you all right?" he pushed out through gritted teeth.

She looked up at him and her face relaxed. "I'm wonderful. How are you?"

He had to stop himself from shaking his head. Only Tabbie would be worried about him. "Perfect."

Slowly, he began moving inside her. Her arms laced around his neck, fingers twined in his hair. As he moved, she whispered words of encouragement, affection, and then desire. Never had a woman wrapped him in a web such as this.

He was spinning toward the end, crashing into love. His love was deepening and strengthening as they spiraled toward bliss. His lips found hers and kissed her between words, wanting to touch every place on her body that he could.

Never had it been like this. This was not a physical act, but an emotional one. If he thought himself bound to Tabbie before, making love to her sealed his fate. He could never be without her. He was hers, forever.

That thought pushed him over the edge, he lost what little control he maintained just as she cried out his name, her body spasming around his.

Rolling to the side, he pulled her against himself. He kissed her hair, her cheeks, her neck. His hands traced every curve, as though he was imprinting this memory forever.

"I might never want to leave this bed," she murmured, tucking her face into the crook of his neck.

He gave a little laugh, tracing his fingers down her spine. "I am in complete agreement. But we'll be boarding a ship in the morning."

He felt her still, tense really. "I thought we were travelling on land to Norfolk."

He squeezed her closer. He'd meant to tell her this before they'd been intimate. He didn't want any confusion on the matter. "I want to stop in London first."

She tried to pull away but he held her. She pushed harder but he refused to let go and then she began slapping at his chest and his face, but still he held on.

He did nothing to protect himself, his face would recover from any damage she did, but he had to keep her by his side or else, something deep in his chest feared he would lose her forever.

Finally, her onslaught slowed. His hand relaxed slightly around her back and that was when she slumped against him. "Will you return to your town house?" He heard her breath catch on the words as though she were trying not to cry.

"I thought we might return to our town house for the short time we were in London." He dared to remove one of his hands from her back to cup her face so that he might lift it and look her in the eyes.

"Don't try to placate me. Just tell me you won't leave me destitute, whatever you intend." A tear slid down her cheek.

"Destitute?" He'd laugh if it didn't seem so serious. "I intend to fill your belly with my child and then stuff your mouth with anything you wish to eat and wrap your body in whatever you'd like to wear and then build you the home you've always dreamed of living in."

Her eyes blinked several times before she choked out. "You're not finished with me?"

"Finished?" How could she even think that? "Tabbie, we've barely begun."

"Then why are we going to London? That is the place for you to be a rake."

And then he understood. All those times she'd tensed when they had discussed London. "We can live anywhere in the world you wish, including London. I'll never be that man again. The geography is irrelevant. I need more than just physical pleasure, my moon goddess. I need your love." He kissed her long and hard. "And I thought you needed your family. It was my intention that we try to make amends with them before we settle in the country."

Two more tears slipped down her cheeks before she buried her face again. "I'm such a fool. An impulsive, silly fool."

He shushed her tears, "You've every right to be suspicious of me. It will take time but I'll prove my devotion to you."

"Did I hurt you?" She choked again as her head came up.

"No love, though if any woman could, it would be you." He snuggled her closer. "Get some rest."

CHAPTER 9

Three days had passed since their wedding and Luke now sat in the parlor awaiting an audience with the Duke of Waverly.

His father-in-law was keeping him waiting.

Tabbie had left to speak with the duchess. They had discussed it and Tabbie was sure her mother was the answer if her father refused to accept the marriage. He grinned. It was yet another of their schemes.

Merciful heaven, he loved that woman. She was glorious as she came up with a tactical plan. And he was glad they had come back to London, even if her father refused to acknowledge the marriage. She needed to see that they could thrive here. Not for his sake but for hers. He knew she would want to continue her work helping women and children, and London was the best place for her to do it. He didn't hold quite the same say as her father did, but he'd be able use his seat on the parliament to further her agenda.

Nothing would make him happier.

Other than her. She made him gloriously happy.

The butler finally appeared. "His Grace will see you now."

Standing, he walked confidently into the library, which seemed to be the duke's preferred place to work.

The other man stood from his desk but gave no other acknowledgement that Luke had entered.

Luke knew some groveling was going to be in order. "Your Grace."

"Sussex," the man barely mumbled.

Luke looked around. "May I ask you a question?"

The man gave a tiny nod.

"Why work in the library? I'm sure you have your choice of rooms." Luke watched as the duke's eyes opened wide in surprise.

"It holds most of the reference materials I need." The Duke cleared his throat looking away.

Just then, a door opened to the left and Tricia appeared. Her eyes also went wide at the sight of him. "Forgive me, Papa," she murmured as she backed out of the room.

Luke grinned. "You don't work in the library because your family enters and exits often?"

The duke cleared his throat. "What is your point?"

"She misses you already. And she's torn up with worry that she won't have a relationship with you."

He saw the duke's face spasm in pain. The man was a horse's ass about having every detail go his way, but he clearly loved his daughter. "She should have thought of that before she eloped."

"She did. But Crummell was an intolerable choice."

Waverly's lip curled. "A week ago, you were an intolerable choice. That girl refuses to heel."

"She is a woman and her refusal to heel is now my concern. I have removed the duty from you." Luke winced. That argument was a double-edged sword. It reminded the duke of his own disobedience in stealing the man's daughter. "I understand Tabbie far better than Crummell ever could."

"She called you a rake and a debaucher—"

"Both were true." Luke leaned back in his chair, unfazed.

"And what will you do when she catches you in the act? She's got quite the temper." The duke's hands were spread across his desk as though he were steadying himself.

"I am aware of her temper and I've no intention of participating in such behavior. I love your daughter. She makes me want to be a better man."

The duke pushed up slightly in his seat. "So you stole her away from her family?"

Luke grimaced. "You've every right to think that. I want to make amends." He cleared his throat. "Perhaps we can marry again in the Church of England. I can only assume you've kept our trip secret. Post the banns and we'll marry for all of society to see."

Waverly sat back in his chair, his hands relaxing on the desk. "I would consider that acceptable. She will move back in to my home and will act the part of an unmarried woman."

Luke felt a twinge of fear. Tabbie was a schemer by nature and that trait likely came from her father. "I will agree to that if you post the banns today and we are married in two weeks' time."

"Absolutely not. I will post the banns but the wedding will take place in three months. I don't want anyone to assume you've ruined her."

"A month, no more. It's possible she is carrying my child, I won't wait any longer."

The duke released a rumble from deep in his chest. "A month. But during that time she will attend all social engagements with us."

"I will agree to that as long as I am in attendance as well." No one knew better than him how base men could be. He'd be damned if he'd let another man touch her.

"Very well," Waverly pushed the marriage contract across the desk. Luke scanned it for any changes.

"I have one more provision," Luke set the paper and pen aside. "Place her dowry in a fund in her name. It's hers to do whatever she'd like with. I will match the funds. In exchange, I'd like to stay here for the next month."

The duke's eyes opened wide. "If you think to visit her room at night while I sleep—"

Luke shook his head. "I won't. But you know that Tabbie is concerned about my previous reputation. She will be eaten with worry if I am staying in my own townhouse. I can assure you, you won't even know I am here."

The duke assessed him. "I have a room in the servants' quarters—"

"Fine," Luke fired back.

"You would sleep in the servants' quarters?" Surprise laced the other man's voice.

Luke pinned the duke with his stare. "I would stay in hell if Tabbie needed me to."

The duke crossed out several lines on the contract and scrolled above them. Then he passed the papers to Luke. Scanning the document, he signed his name. It was done.

"I should have added as a provision that you aid me in future negotiations. I know you've done well for yourself." The duke signed his own name, his features softening.

"I doubt you need my help, Your Grace. But as your son-in-law, I will do so anytime."

"Call me, Henry, son." Waverly stood and extended his hand. "Welcome to the family."

* * *

"He did what?" Tabbie tried to close her mouth but it refused to shut. Her father had called him *son*? Allowed Luke to call him Henry? Only her mother and the Prince Regent used his given name.

He reached for her hand. "The lack of intimacy will be difficult, but at least we will be together."

She sniffed. "I've no intention of following that rule."

"Tabbie, I gave my word." Luke pulled her closer. His smell tickled her nose in the most delightful way. She'd never tire of the feel of him, the smell.

"Actually, you agreed that you wouldn't visit my room, you never said you wouldn't entertain me in yours." She wrapped her arms around his neck.

He dropped his lips to her hair. "My scheming moon goddess," he murmured chuckling. "Leave it to you to find the loophole."

Leaning back she gave him a brilliant smile. "Thank you for making this right with my father and for understanding my fears. I don't know what more I could have asked for in a husband."

He bent down to press his lips to hers. As usual, all thought left her head at the touch of his lips. "I am afraid you will have to suffer my absence occasionally."

"Why?" She hated the worry in her voice.

"I've decided to take a more active role in parliament. I know we will move to my country estate, but I'm sure you'll want to continue your work and I can't help you if I'm not part of the government."

Her eyes went wide and her mouth dropped open again. Then her lips found his and nothing else mattered. "I love you," she finally managed to whisper.

"And I you, my moon goddess."

EPILOGUE

Tabbie lay in bed, warm and snug despite the driving rain soaking the London streets. They'd come to the city far earlier than intended. Parliament didn't begin for another month, but Luke didn't want to wait any longer to make the journey.

Not with their second child on the way.

Luke stirred behind her. She turned her face to give her husband a smile. "It's time to get up. I just heard the clock chime seven."

He groaned. "I'm not going out today. I am staying in bed with my wife."

"You promised my father you'd aid him in the negotiations." But she snuggled deeper. His hands were splayed out across her belly as he kissed her neck.

"Papa," little Henry called from the door. "Mama?"

"Come in, darling," she called and pulled back the covers for their son to join them. He was nearly three and the spitting image of his father.

He scooted into the bed with them. "It's waining," he gave them a sleepy smile as he too snuggled deeper.

"That decides it," Luke rumbled behind her. "I declare this day a Sussex family holiday. We're staying in bed, the lot of us."

Tabbie smiled, leaning back to kiss her husband. He'd made good on each of his promises. In the four years they'd been married, they'd never spent a night apart. Not even in her father's house. No matter where they were, London, Norfolk, Scotland, his eyes were for her alone. Her fears had died some time ago.

A carriage rumbled on the street below. Henry hopped from the bed and ran to the window. "It's Grandpapa!" He danced a little jig and ran for the door.

"What in the bloody blue blazes is your father doing here at seven in the morning?" Luke groused behind her, still holding her against his body, his hands searching for baby parts across her belly.

"He knows if he doesn't collect you, you won't come." She grinned, thankful he couldn't see it. Her father shamelessly abused Luke's feelings for her on more than one occasion. He knew Luke would go today, not for his father-in-law's sake, but for Tabbie's.

Luke harrumphed. "If I am to spend the day engaged in your father's business affairs, you have to entertain my parents. They can't get enough of Henry."

"Done," she grinned. "I'll send a missive for you by four so that my father doesn't keep you all evening."

"Swear it." He kissed her long and hard. "I want to be home with my family for the evening meal and my wife tucked into bed with me by eight."

"Eight?" she cried her eyes twinkling. "What happened to that rake who stayed out all hours of the evening?"

"Oh, he's still here." Luke gave her a wicked grin. "I might want you in bed but I didn't say anything about sleeping."

Her breath caught. He still did that to her after four years. "Promise," she said as her lips found his.

"Tabbie," it came out as a growl. "If you kiss me like that again, your father is going to be waiting for a very long time."

"Promise," she whispered again. Her rake was absolutely perfect.

Did you love Tabbie and Luke? Want to hear more about them? They are both major characters in the follow up novella My Duke's Seduction! Wicked Lords of London is a new series that begins with the Earl of Sussex. My Duke's Seduction features, Tricia, Tabbies' sister and a duke who is absolutely certain he doesn't want such a troublesome bride! http://amzn.to/2CuT9a3

ALSO IN THE WICKED EARLS' CLUB

Earl of Sussex http://amzn.to/2CLa1xp
Earl of Westcliff http://amzn.to/2CFE3l7
Earl of Wainthorpe http://amzn.to/2CtbGTY
Earl of Sunderland http://amzn.to/2CWYAj3
Earl of Basingstoke http://amzn.to/2AuNE9z
Earl of Weston http://amzn.to/2CWt30w
Earl of Davenport http://amzn.to/2CIcPKA
Earl of Grayson http://amzn.to/2CW1t3x
Earl of Benton http://amzn.to/2qyR5wf
Earl of Pembroke http://amzn.to/2CJun9s
Earl of St. Seville http://amzn.to/2qwbfXw
Earl of Harrington http://amzn.to/2Cs1Fq3

CHRISTMASTIDE WITH THE CAPTAIN

Christmastide with the Captain
  A Laird to Love Prequel

By Tammy Andresen

Emilia stood on the beach, despite the biting wind and misty air that December inevitably brought. Her hands smarted from the cold but she embraced the sensation, adding it to the list of reasons why self-pity was the emotion most likely to propel her through Christmastide.

They were all going to marry. Each one of her cousins and sisters had fallen hopelessly in love over the last year and were either married or about to be. And poor, quiet, bookish Emilia was going to be left alone in this drafty Scottish castle. Who was ever going to love her?

The grey water churned bits of white foam mirroring her mood. Perhaps she should join a nunnery. Devote herself to God and charity.

Sitting down in the sand, she allowed her head to drop onto her arms. It was not usually her custom to be so despondent but with the Twelfthtide approaching and her happily coupled family about to arrive, she couldn't help but feel despair. She'd have to face them all alone. Their looks would be pitying, their happiness underscoring her own loneliness.

She'd give anything for those she loved and she didn't begrudge them a single bit. She just wanted a little sliver of hope for herself. Was that wrong? She sent up a silent prayer that she too would find joy in love.

But her plea was cut short. Out of the mist a booming noise sounded across the water. Her head snapped up as the vague outline of a ship came into view.

But something was wrong, the ship listed at an angle and didn't correct itself as the waves rolled.

Standing, Emilia craned her neck to get a better view but her blonde hair blew into her face. Swishing it away, she lifted her skirts to step closer to the grey water. As the ship moved closer, its outline grew clearer. It was in distress. The sails hung limply as the ship tipped at an even wilder angle to the water. Gasping into the wind, she forced her legs to move as she raced along the beach. She threw open the door to the lighthouse and climbed the narrow stairs.

It was slow going thanks to her morning dress, but she lifted it higher and made her way to the top. Sounding the bell that alerted the castle above, she lit the lamp and prayed the ship would see its light. Then back down the stairs she flew, out the door and across the beach where several rowboats were moored.

If she'd stopped to think, she'd have realized that a single rowboat could not possibly hold an entire crew, but fear propelled her as Emilia climbed onto one of the dinghies and began rowing out to the ship. She heard the chains as it dropped anchor and then the whizzing of the ropes as several other dinghies dropped from the deck into the ocean but her eyes were on the shore as she pushed the boat out past the break to aid the failing vessel.

A rowboat passed her by and one of the sailors being shuttled to the shore called out. "You're a woman." As if that was somehow significant.

"Thank ye for noticing," she huffed back. It would have been far better if she'd been able to deliver it with a good measure of disdain but alas, she was running out of breath.

Another dinghy passed by and she stopped for a moment to check behind and see if everyone was off the ship. It seemed prudent to turn around if they were. Much of her fear had been replaced with exhaustion.

One more dinghy made its way towards her, laden down with men. She watched in horror as a massive wave rolled toward them. With so many men, they were powerless to move out of the way and too heavy to roll atop the wall of water. It took them over, crashing the men into the ocean.

She might have screamed, but the wind ripped it away and then she redoubled her efforts, rolling easily over the massive wave and pushing toward the men who were now bobbing helplessly in the water.

She rowed toward them until she reached the first man attempting to stay above the water and, holding out an oar, she yelled, "Get in!" Reaching out her hand, she helped him climb into the rowboat. He collapsed on the bottom of the tiny ship and then she collected another swimming toward the shore. The overturned dinghy had landed right side up and several men were crawling back into it as well.

Between Emilia's boat and the other dinghy, all the men save one had been pulled from the ocean and she made her way to where he tread water.

When she reached down her oar, the man latched onto it, his blue eyes piercing into hers in a way that made her already labored breath rush out of her chest. They were so mesmerizing she completely forgot to reach out her hand to help in into the boat.

He climbed up anyway, grasping the side of the ship, and then several men reached over to pull him into the nearly full dinghy.

Unlike many of the men who had collapsed into the boat, the second his feet hit the bottom, he stood. Without missing a breath, he grasped her about the waist and hauled her up against him. She nearly dropped the oars in her surprise. For a moment, she had a wild thought that he would kiss her. Her eyes widened as his held hers captive. Every nerve tingled as she became aware of all the places his hard body pressed against hers.

Her lips parted in anticipation but he only gave her a small smile and then his hands left her waist as he slipped underneath her arm, sitting on the bench behind her. Grasping her waist again, he pulled her down into his lap.

Confusion knitted her brow and she turned back to look at him. "Sir, what are you—"

The smile returned as his hand came over hers, to clasp the oars. "I thought I might help you row." His breath was warm against her cheek and it made her tingle in the strangest places.

"Oh," she exclaimed as his hands grasped hers on the oars. Then he began to move, her body cradled into his as she worked with him to row the boat back to shore.

A flush climbed her cheeks as they swayed back and forth, their bodies moving together. She'd never been this close to a man, so intimately entwined, and her body hummed with the feel of it. If not for the cold seeping into every extremity, it might have been the most exciting moment of her life.

The waves helped push them onto the beach and the men hopped out, pulling the rowboat further onto the shore. Without a word, the man whose lap she sat upon stood and swept her into his arms. Deftly he climbed over the side of the boat and then began making his way up the beach, still holding her.

"Lady Emilia," one of the stablemen, Creeves, called out from the bottom of the stairs. He must have seen the light or heard the bell and had come to aid the ship. "Are you all right, my lady?"

"My lady?" His voice whispered into her ear.

She turned to look at him, which might have been a mistake, because then her lips were just a breath away from his. She wondered what they might taste like. Salt, of course. He'd just been in the ocean. Blinking, she tried to clear those thoughts. "Y-y-yes. I-I am-m-m the d-d-daughter…" What was wrong with her voice? Belatedly she realized she was shivering despite his heat.

"It's all right, you can tell me later. I am Captain Jack Andrews. I owe you a debt of gratitude for aiding us. You saved my men's life today as well as my own."

She gave a nod as more of the servants began flooding onto the beach. Voices were calling from everywhere, questions were being bandied about from all directions but she could barely understand them as she shrank further down into Captain Andrew's heat.

Her head lolled onto his shoulder and her eyes drifted closed. "No sleeping now," his voice called her back.

"H-h-how are y-y-y-you still s-s-s-tanding?" she managed to ask between shivers. His clothes were soaked through and dripping.

"I am used to being wet and cold. But you, my lady, need to get inside." He barked several orders to his crew and her staff and then he began climbing the steps off the beach and up to her home two at a time.

Either she was too cold to care, or he was exceptionally gentle, because she'd barely noticed any jostling as they climbed. Quite suddenly, they were at the top and he was striding toward the castle. Dimly she was aware of Creeves next to them, panting with the effort it took him to keep pace. "Captain," he gasped. "Should I run ahead and tell 'em yer comin'?"

"No need," he said. She felt a tiny rumble of laughter in his chest and despite the cold, her lips turned up a little. Creeves had gone mad if he thought he'd outpace the captain to the door.

"I-I c-can walk," she pushed past her lips, her tremor lessening as they moved away from the beach and the strong wind that bit at the shore.

"I'll hold you," he murmured, his lips vibrating against the top of her head. "I'll have you inside in a moment and tucked into a nice warm bed."

Bed. The word hummed through her head as images of the captain in her room, laying her on her bed, flitted through her mind. Places she'd never even been aware of heated at his words. More thoughts of their bodies pressed together, their clothes falling away, their mouths…

"Emilia," her father's voice boomed over the courtyard, interrupting her train of thought entirely.

Captain Andrews quickened his pace yet again, leaving Creeves behind. "She is very cold, my lord. She needs to get inside."

"This way." Her father turned as they came beside him and began walking toward the front door. "I trust you'll give me a full accounting of what has happened."

Emilia tried to lift her head to reply but before she could even think the words, the captain was answering. "Of course, my lord. I've twenty wet and frightened men on the beach. Do you have anywhere I might dry and warm them?"

Her father's deep brogue bellowed for all to hear. "Bring 'em intae the main hall."

"Thank you, my lord," the captain replied as he strode through the double doors, the warmth of the castle touching her skin. With a sigh, she closed her eyes again.

* * *

"No sleeping," Jack looked down at the lovely woman curled in his arms. He'd strip her down himself and hold her close to warm her freezing skin, consequences be damned, if that was what it took to save her. He owed her nothing less after what she had done for him and his men.

Her lashes fluttered open again, revealing the deep pools of her green eyes. Her gaze was confused as she looked up at him, her sweet mouth puckering in the most delightful way. "Sleep?" she murmured.

"That's right. Stay awake for me now, my lady. Emilia, is it?" He gave her a smile that felt forced, even to him. In all honestly, he was frightened. More so than he'd been out on the ocean or even when the dinghy had tipped. He'd long ago deemed his own life expendable. Worth little or nothing. But she was another matter entirely. Any woman strong enough to toss herself out onto the open ocean to save a group of strangers deserved all the best life had to offer.

"Mmhhh," she replied slowly. "You're warm."

This time the tugging up of his lips was genuine rather than forced. "And you are quite beautiful."

Her eyes opened wider then. "That's kind." Her head lolled to the side as though she were drunk.

He jostled her in his arms as her father led him up the stairs. It wasn't meant to be kind, it was the truth. "You doubt my words?" he asked a good deal louder than necessary.

Her head came back up. "My sisters are beautiful. Fiona has flaming red hair as wild as her spirit…" Her voice drifted off again.

"Sisters? How many?" he asked, mostly to keep her talking.

"Two," she murmured.

"And who is the other?"

"Ainsley. Everyone loves Ainsley. Everywhere she goes people tell her…" Her voice began to fade and her father looked back at them. He was a large man with hair that looked as though it had been quite red, but was now streaked with grey. Everything about him commanded respect, except his eyes. They were filled with worry. Jack was sure his own gaze mirrored the emotion.

"What do people tell Ainsley?" Even to his own tongue, it felt strange to use their given names but he'd do anything to keep her talking.

"How charming she is. So accomplished." Her head lifted. "And my cousin, Clarissa, you'd like her. She's English."

His eyebrow quirked. She had clearly identified his accent as English though he had no idea why that meant he might like her cousin. He disliked a good many English men and women. Besides, he was at least half Scot. The other half was another matter entirely.

"Does she go around saving ships full of sailors too?" He gave her another little jostle just to keep her awake.

Jack heard her father grunt. "She didna'."

"I didn't save you. You mostly saved me." She snuggled closer.

He had the most ridiculous urge to kiss the top of her head, her cheeks, her eyes. "I believe it was you who fished me out of the water."

Her father opened a door up ahead and stepped into the room. Jack followed. The room would have made him grin if he wasn't so worried. Books were stacked on every surface, cozy blankets draped across each of the chairs, a fire crackled in the hearth. Not pausing to ask permission, he strode over to it and dropped to his knees. "That feels so good," she near moaned, her face turning to the flames.

His body clenched at the sound of her breathy voice. Was he responding to her? Damnation, this wasn't the time to desire a woman. He gave his head a shake, trying to clear it.

Three maids entered the room and for a moment, he held her closer to his body, savoring the feel of her before she was taken away.

Want to read more? Find Christmastide with my Captain: A Laird to Love http://amzn.to/2CxGMKh

Or you can view the entire A Laird to Love series:

My Enemy, My Earl: A Laird to Love Book 1 http://amzn.to/2F2jY7c

Heart of a Highlander: A Laird to Love Book 2 http://amzn.to/2CxIgnP

A Scot's Surrender: A Laird to Love Book 3 http://amzn.to/2CIGWSj

My Laird's Seduction: A Laird to Love Book 4

EARL OF WESTCLIFF

The Wicked Earls' Club
THE BRAYDENS
Meara Platt

Tynan Brayden, the sixth Earl of Westcliff, peered out of the window of his club onto Bedford Place, knowing he had a choice to make – either remove the last of his clothing and join the beautiful viscountess who was already naked in his bed, eager to share a night of pleasure with him – or leave his bedchamber to discover the identity of the young woman draped in moonlight who was standing alone across the street from his club for the third night in a row and find out what she was doing there.

Was there a doubt of his decision?

He eyed the strawberries and cream, the peacock feather, and the black silk ribbons sitting atop his bureau and sighed. "We'll have to do this another night, Daniella. Something has just come up." He intended no pun by his remark, nor was the viscountess clever enough to understand the double meaning in his words.

"Is it my husband?" Daniella, Lady Bascom, leaped from his

bed and hastily tossed on her elegant silk gown. "He must have returned to London early. Or never left at all. Why, that deceitful liar! He must have hired Bow Street runners to follow me." She gathered up the undergarments she'd removed moments earlier and fled from his room without giving him so much as a passing glance.

"Have a good evening," Tynan muttered as she slammed the door behind her. In truth, he was relieved. Their nights, despite the sex games she often enjoyed playing, had grown quite dull and unsatisfying to him. Intimacy, he supposed, required the participating parties to actually feel something for each other. Something more than indifference.

He returned his attention to the young lady who stood alone on the street, no sign of her driver or carriage this evening, which left her easy prey for any passerby who wished to take advantage. Out there, she was vulnerable. A lost rabbit among a pack of wolves.

"Bollocks." Three of those wolves had just spotted her and were now about to circle her.

He grabbed his boots, quickly stuffing his feet into them, and at the same time glancing around for the shirt he'd removed only moments ago. Daniella, he realized, must have scooped it up along with her undergarments in her mad rush to flee his chamber. There was no time to grab another, for those three not so fine gentlemen were dangerously close to his little rabbit, eyeing her for their next meal. *His little rabbit?* No, he didn't know the girl and had no intention of getting involved beyond rescuing her from this scrape.

Tynan knew he had to move fast. By the sidelong glances these men were casting her, and their sudden whispers to each other, they were about to make their move.

He reached for his pistols and hurried downstairs, hoping to make it out of the club and across the street before the girl was harmed. Not that he should care or feel protective of her in any way. Or that he should still nonsensically be thinking of her as *his* little rabbit. Where was her family? Did no one notice her missing?

There was a chill to the air on this October evening, a hint of upcoming winter. Tynan felt the wind's cool prickle against his chest the moment he stepped out of his club. "You there... girl." He didn't know what to call her. My darling bunny was not at all appropriate. Was she married? A spinster? No, she looked too young to be on the shelf. But not too young to know better than to be traipsing about London alone at night. "Get behind me."

She frowned at him. "Do I know you, sir?"

"No, nor do I believe you know those three gentlemen who are eyeing you for dessert." He turned to the three obviously inebriated men and trained his pistols on them. "Take another step toward the girl and it shall be your last."

"No need for that, m'lord," said their leader, an arrogant fellow with a cruel smile and an avid gleam in his eyes that revealed his less than honorable intentions toward the girl. He had no business here. Not that this was one of the finer London neighborhoods, but neither was it anywhere near the worst. The townhouses on Bedford Place were neatly maintained and might have been considered elegant if not for their occupants who were mostly mistresses and courtesans who plied their trade to a fashionable clientele. "We're willin' to share her with you."

The girl scurried to Tynan's side. "I am indebted to you, sir. I hadn't noticed them. I'm glad you did."

Her voice was soft and lilting.

He caught the scent of roses on her skin, with a subtle hint of lemon and summer sunshine mixed in.

She was prettier than he'd expected, but he dared not take his gaze off the blackguards, not while they were obviously mulling how best to overpower him and grab the girl. "Get inside," he ordered her. "You'll be safe with me. I give you my word of honor."

She hesitated.

"I have no wish to spill blood, but these gentlemen are determined to have you. I'll be forced to shoot them if you continue to stand here and provide temptation."

"Oh, I see." She stepped into the club.

He backed in after her, his gaze and pistols trained on the men who were not at all pleased that their little rabbit had just gotten away. He shoved the door closed and called for two passing footmen to stand guard. "Keep weapons at hand. We might have trouble from those drunken fools tonight."

They both nodded. "Aye, m'lord."

"Has Lord Coventry arrived yet? Or Sussex or Wainthorpe?"

"No, m'lord," the older footman said. "Nor any of the other earls."

"When they do arrive, warn them to remain alert." He waited for these trusted retainers to take their positions by the door, and then turned scowling toward the girl. "Are you attics to let? Where is your driver? More important, why have you been standing across the street, scouting this building for the past three nights?"

When she did not deign to respond, he tucked the smaller pistol into its holster in his boot, grabbed her hand, and attempted to haul her upstairs to his quarters. She stood her ground and fought back, determined to shove away from him. "Unhand me!"

"Not until I have my answers." Having no patience for her resistance, he lifted her over his shoulder.

She gasped and pounded on his back. "You gave me your word of honor! Where are you taking me?"

"Somewhere we can continue this discussion in private." He did not particularly care who saw her, but the lords and ladies who frequented the Wicked Earls' Club expected discretion and could not afford to be seen by her... whoever she was.

He marched into his chamber and shut the door behind them, ignoring her startled cry as the latch fell into place. He set her down in the center of the room and moved away, for she was obviously scared of him and he needed to calm her down. "What is your business here?"

"You wretch!"

He growled when she unexpectedly kicked his shin and tried to dodge around him to reach the door.

He grabbed her by the waist and drew her up against him, his intention merely to prevent her escape. To his surprise, she felt soft and wonderful. He released her, but made certain to stand between her and the door. "Why did you kick me?"

Instead of replying, she fumbled through her reticule and withdrew her own pistol. With a small, trembling hand, she pointed it at him. "You assured me that I would be safe with you."

"Put that thing down before you hurt yourself." He moved toward his desk and set his own pistol down on it. "You are safe with me. I have no interest in making you my next bed partner." Although he'd just gotten a good look at the girl and - *holy hell* - she was beautiful. Auburn hair that was lush and silky, and hinting of curls that were too unruly to ever properly behave. Big amber-brown eyes that were the vibrant color of expensive brandy. And a body that had his heart pounding so hard, it almost dropped him to his knees.

He doubted that she trusted him, and in this moment, he wasn't certain that he could be trusted with her.

Her lips were tantalizingly soft and pink. He'd been too busy staring at them to realize she'd lowered her weapon. "I may as well introduce myself. Tynan Brayden, Earl of Westcliff, at your service."

Her lips puckered as he gave a mock bow. "An earl," she said, placing emphasis on his title. "My goodness."

He arched an eyebrow, relieved when she finally stuck the pistol back in her reticule. He noted that her hands were still trembling. "Your turn," he said, purposely keeping his voice gentle. "Who are you?"

"No one of consequence, I assure you. Lady Abigail Croft. My brother is Peter Croft, Baron Whitpool. His is an old title, but that's about all that can be said for the good. In truth, I feel it is more of a family curse."

He could hear the heartbreak in her every word.

"I wasn't here because of your club." Her release of breath came out in a ragged and rather forlorn sigh. "I was trying to work up the courage to enter the house next door. It is where my brother goes nightly... for his... to forget about the demons that haunt him."

Any irritation he might have felt toward the girl's folly had now fled. If Tynan understood her correctly, her brother was an addict. Bollocks, that was trouble. He and his fellow earls had become increasingly concerned by the fashionable artists salon next door that had lately turned into something more sinister. The place was frequented by romantic poets, many of whom were darlings of the *ton*. Someone in very high authority shielded them, perhaps not realizing this house was more of an opium den than a salon for patrons of enlightened literature. "I'm truly sorry, Lady Abigail. How long has this been going on with your brother?"

"Ever since he returned home from the war. He was recalled from his regiment when he came into the title last year. But his condition has gotten especially bad these past few months. Perhaps he's been like this for years and I hadn't noticed until now. He was wounded years ago in Spain fighting Napoleon's forces, you see."

Tynan regarded her with concern. "He was a soldier?"

She clasped her hands together, wringing them as she nodded. "The youngest of four sons, so it was either fighting or the clergy for him. He chose fighting." She cast Tynan a wincing smile. "I love him, but Peter was never the pious sort. My parents knew it, too. As for me, I was the accidental fifth child, the girl they had hoped for and finally got. Being the only girl among all those boys, and the youngest as well, I was either picked on mercilessly or worshiped. There was never a middle ground."

If she had four older brothers, then where were the other three? Why was she left the task of bringing Peter home? It made no sense.

She cleared her throat. "My lord, have you lost your shirt?"

"What?" He glanced down, noting he was clad only in his trousers and boots, and only now recalling he'd run out in this state of undress. He kept a wardrobe at his club, but he'd been too distracted by the girl to bother making himself respectable. Was it necessary? She was in his chamber. Alone with him. They were strangers to each other. There was nothing respectable about their situation. "Give me a moment."

He fetched a clean shirt and slipped it on, buttoning it only part way up and rolling up his shirt sleeves since he wasn't going to fumble with cufflinks or don a bloody cravat, vest, or jacket for her sake. In truth, there was a sensual innocence about the girl that made him think of shedding clothes - mainly hers - rather than tediously putting his on.

Her gown was seductively prim, he noticed. A dark blue woolen weave with a white lace collar that buttoned to her throat. A man would have to work for hours to slip that gown off her slender shoulders. He ran his gaze up and down her body once more. Ah, but she'd be worth every bit of the effort it would take to peel those layers off her. "I'm afraid I cannot leave my club yet, Lady Abigail. If you promise not to run off the moment my back is turned, I'll have my carriage brought around to take you home."

She nodded. "I give you my word. Thank you. This was my driver's night off and I foolishly thought... well, clearly I wasn't thinking. I'd hired a hack and paid the driver to wait for me, but the horrid man disappeared the moment I handed over the money. I was stranded and didn't know what to do."

As though fully realizing just how incredibly idiotic and dangerous her actions had been, she blushed and glanced away.

Her innocent eyes lit up the moment she noticed what was sitting upon his bureau top. "Are those strawberries? And cream?"

Tynan realized she was hungry and not thinking of the games one played in bed with... never mind. "Yes, please have them. I'll ring for some more food to be brought up for you while you await your ride home."

"Oh, no. It isn't necessary. The strawberries are perfect. Thank you." She dipped one in cream, closed her eyes, and tipped her head back to take it into her mouth. Her tongue darted out to lick at a spot of cream that had landed at the corner of her mouth. "Oh, my. This is heavenly."

Holy hell.

Her eyes were still closed while she slowly savored each lush, juicy bite. "Would you care for one, my lord?"

"No, Lady Abigail." His throat was suddenly as tight as the rest of his body. "Have them all. I wouldn't deny you the obvious pleasure."

She opened her eyes and smiled at him in appreciation, a genuinely sincere and warm smile that upended his heart once again.

"Oh, and what a lovely feather."

Bollocks.

"It's a peacock feather, isn't it?"

He wished the girl would keep her hands off those things. In truth, they weren't his. The viscountess had brought the peacock feather and silk bindings along in anticipation of a night of erotic fantasy. Her fantasies. Not his. He was merely her chosen stud bull.

Since he was single, unattached, and feeling particularly restless lately, he'd accepted her proposition. Meaningless sex with a beautiful woman who wanted no commitment.

So why was he relieved that it had not taken place?

Worse, why was he enjoying his night of celibacy with one of the most clueless young women ever to cross his path?

"Oh, what lovely silk ribbons. They're a rich, lustrous black. What are you—"

"Give me those." He grabbed them from her fingers and stuck them in the top drawer of his desk. "I gave you permission to eat my strawberries, not dig through my belongings."

Her eyes rounded in surprise. "The ribbons are yours?"

He cleared his throat that was still so tight, it was a miracle he didn't sound like a bullfrog. "They belong to a friend. None of your business who she is."

"I suppose the peacock feather is hers, too." She held it up against her hair, no doubt believing it was a hair adornment and not... never mind.

"Put that thing down. Where were you raised? In an isolated abbey in the wilds of Yorkshire? Did no one ever teach you manners?"

She glanced up at him in surprise. "Yes, my abbey was in Yorkshire. How did you know?"

He frowned. "But you just told me that you had a family. Four brothers. Parents."

She nodded, her expression suddenly turning pained. "My mother died when I was five. My father passed on shortly afterward. My eldest brother, Thomas, became Baron Whitpool. He tried to keep us all together, but couldn't manage us and the Whitpool properties, all of which were run down and plagued with debt. I was too young to help out, and my other three brothers were terrors even when under our parents' strict supervision."

She paused a moment and glanced around. "My lord, may I sit?"

"Of course. Forgive my rudeness."

However, before he had a chance to pull out the lone chair that was situated behind his writing desk, she sank onto his bed and released a breathy sigh. "Thomas married a girl from a wealthy, local family," she said, her slender shoulders sagging from the weight of her obvious unhappiness. "He hoped she would help him restore order to the Whitpool household. She did, by shipping me off to the abbey. I remained there until I was sixteen."

"How long ago was that?"

Her big, sad eyes met his stern gaze. "Are you asking me how old I am?"

He folded his arms across his chest, needing to do something to distract him from the heat flowing through his veins and the inexplicable urge to hold her in his arms and protect her forever. Perhaps he was the one who needed protection from her. He turned away and grabbed his vest, putting it on as he answered her question. The more layers between them, the better. "I just saved your life. I deserve some answers."

She nodded. "I suppose you do. I'm twenty years old. My brother, Thomas, died when I was sixteen. Childless. So his horrid ogre of a wife returned to her family and William became the new Baron Whitpool. He brought me back home. By then, he and our other brother, Gideon, had established a shipping company that hauled freight back and forth from the West Indies. Sugar. Spices. Rum."

"They must have been successful businessmen." He'd learned much in running the Westcliff properties as well as assisting to run this establishment. Even if one hired excellent managers, there was no substitute for one's own diligence and attentiveness.

"Yes, they were. William never gave up his love of the sea. Despite his baronial responsibilities, he often joined Gideon on the shorter trips, sometimes to Ireland and sometimes to Flanders. They were caught last year in a sudden squall off the Irish Sea." Her voice turned tremulous and raspy. "Both of my brothers drowned."

He didn't know what to say. So many losses in so short a span of time. He had three brothers of his own and could not imagine how he would have handled losing any of them. He felt a sudden pang of remorse. He hadn't seen his family in a while. Perhaps he would stop by his mother's townhouse for an overdue visit.

Perhaps he'd invite this girl along when he did. "I'm so sorry, Abigail. Truly."

"Thank you, my lord."

"No, call me Tynan. Or just Ty." That's what his brothers called him when they weren't calling him something worse. They all loved each other, but they were brothers, after all. How else were they to show their love if not by mercilessly pounding on each other? "Call me whatever you wish."

He did not bother with formality.

There was no propriety to their situation, especially not now with her sitting atop the silk sheets of his four-poster bed. He dragged the chair out from behind his desk and moved it near the bed. Turning it around, he rested his arms on its high back and sat straddling the seat so that he could face her.

The chair's high back served as a barrier between them.

A necessary barrier, for she'd somehow stripped away his irritation. All he wanted to do was take her in his arms and comfort her.

In truth, he wanted to do much more.

But he wasn't going to touch her. He'd promised.

She looked as soft and vulnerable as a gentle rabbit. *His little rabbit.* But he liked that she was also strong and spirited, ready to fight to save her last surviving brother. "Tell me more about Peter."

What he really wanted to know was more about her.

Every blessed thing he could learn about her.

She curled her hands around the bedpost, as though the sad memories had cast her adrift and she needed to hold onto something solid that would serve as her anchor. "There isn't much more to tell. He came home to take over the title and its responsibilities, but he'd been wounded during his military service and remains in terrible pain. The wounds never mended properly. No matter what the doctors have done to try to heal him, he awakens each morning in agony."

"That's how he ended up next door," Tynan said, his voice barely above a murmur. "Each night he goes to that opium den to relieve the tormenting pain."

She released a breath and nodded. "I want to take him home. I want to get him to the Whitpool estate by the seashore that he loves so much. I want to get him away from London and the bad influence of his friends. But I can't do it alone and no one will help me."

She gazed at him with her big, brandy-colored eyes.

Bollocks.

He only needed to give a responsive nod in sympathy. She wasn't asking for his help. She was merely relating her tale of woe.

"Abigail..." *Shut up, you idiot.*

"Yes, my lord?"

He groaned.

What tempest was he about to sail into?

Want to read more? Find the Earl of Westcliff and ten other Wicked Earls on all major retailers. http://amzn.to/2CFE3l7

ABOUT Meara

Meara Platt is a USA Today bestselling author and an award winning, Amazon UK All-star. Her favorite place in all the world is England's Lake District, which may not come as a surprise since many of her stories are set in that idyllic landscape, including her Romance Writers of America Golden Heart award winning story released as Book 3 in her paranormal romance Dark Gardens series. If you'd like to learn more about the ancient Fae prophecy that is about to unfold in the Dark Gardens series, as well as Meara's lighthearted, international bestselling Regency romances in the Farthingale Series, please visit Meara's website at www.mearaplatt.com.

OTHER TITLES BY TAMMY ANDRESEN

Want a free novella?

https://instafreebie.com/free/M0QWQ

Taming the Duke's Heart
Taming a Duke's Reckless Heart
Taming a Duke's Wild Rose
Taming a Laird's Wild Lady
Taming a Rake into a Lord
Taming a Savage Gentleman
Taming a Rogue Earl

Fairfield Fairy Tales
Stealing a Lady's Heart
Hunting for a Lady's Heart
Entrapping a Lord's Love: Coming in February of 2018

American Historical Romance
Lily in Bloom
Midnight Magic
The Golden Rules of Love

Boxsets!!
Taming the Duke's Heart Books 1-3

Taming the Duke's Heart Books 4-6

American Brides

ABOUT THE AUTHOR

More about Tammy

Tammy Andresen lives with her husband and three children just outside of Boston, Massachusetts. She grew up on the Seacoast of Maine, where she spent countless days dreaming up stories in blueberry fields and among the scrub pines that line the coast. Her mother loved to spin a yarn and Tammy filled many hours listening to her mother retell the classics. It was inevitable that at the age of 18, she headed off to Simmons College, where she studied English literature and education. She never left Massachusetts but some of her heart still resides in Maine and her family visits often.

What the Critics are saying:

"The characters are well-developed and interesting, the plot is edge-of-your-seat intriguing, and the setting is one with so much history. If you are a fan of history mixed with mystery and intrigue, you won't be disappointed." Linda Thompson THE AUTHOR SHOW

"While the relationship between Lily and Eric is the primary focus of this story, the mystery/supense factor is what kept this from being JUST a historical romance. Lily in Bloom was a fast-

paced, romantic read that I absoutely LOVED."
http://alysenovak.blogspot.com

"… it held not only a pure romance but the simple magic that goes with it. I was enchanted with this story from the beginning until the end and I didn't want it to end. I wanted it to go on." Robin

Find out more about Tammy:
http://tammyandresen.com
https://www.facebook.com/authortammyandresen
https://twitter.com/TammyAndresen
https://www.pinterest.com/tammy_andresen/
https://plus.google.com/+TammyAndresen/

Made in the USA
Middletown, DE
01 November 2018